RAIDERS OF SPANISH FLAT

Signing on with Hank Allison's Bar A outfit was probably one of the biggest mistakes Brad Travis had made. No one could have told him that he would soon be drawn into a game of intrigue and skulduggery, where the very air reeked of double-dealing and menace. Allison was being plagued by cow-thieves and Brad had earned a reputation to be reckoned with. He needed all his skill against a gang of rustlers whose law came out of the muzzles of blazing six-shooters.

RAIDERS OF SPANISH FLAT

RAIDERS OF SPANISH FLAT

by
Russ Bowen

Dales Large Print Books
Long Preston, North Yorkshire,
England.

British Library Cataloguing in Publication Data.

Bowen, Russ
    Raiders of Spanish Flat.

    A catalogue record for this book is
    available from the British Library

    ISBN 1-85389-900-3 pbk

First published in Great Britain by Robert Hale Ltd., 1992

Copyright © 1992 by Russ Bowen

Cover illustration © Longarron by arrangement with Norma
Editorial S.A.

The right of Russ Bowen to be identified as the author
of this work has been asserted by him in accordance with
the Copyright, Designs and Patents Act, 1988

Published in Large Print 1999 by arrangement with Robert
Hale Ltd.

Dales Large Print is an imprint of
Library Magna Books Ltd.
Printed and bound in Great Britain by
T.J. International Ltd., Cornwall, PL28 8RW.

One

Brad Travis thought the yellow-haired woman was really something to look at, especially after the long miles of featureless country he had covered to reach this cowtown called Oxbow. She sat on the driving seat of a ranch wagon at the front of Hopper's store and idly flipped at the bothersome flies while, just as idly, she surveyed the panorama presented by the rambling main street.

The face that Brad's gaze lingered on was finely cut, almost patrician, with big wide eyes that just then reflected sheer boredom. The chin was firm and determined, wilful, even; the full red lips had a petulant set. She wore male riding garb, rough pants and blue cotton shirt. Her bare neck was a smooth, tanned column of grace that caused Brad's pulse to beat a trifle faster.

It seemed that the weary clip-clopping of his horse—or perhaps it was the pull of his steady, devouring stare—claimed her wandering attention, and for an instant each eyed the other, curiosity flowing back and forth that presently, for the woman's part, became a hostile challenge.

She snapped her eyes away abruptly and looked towards the store doorway, to where an aproned clerk had appeared with an armful of parcels.

'Want me to put them in the back, Miz Allison?'

'Where else would you put them, Ike? Put them in the back, of course. And mind how you handle the eggs. I hope you have them properly packed this time.'

'Yes, sir, Miz Allison.'

'And, Ike ...'

Her voice was swallowed in the din made by a freight wagon trundling down the road. Brad dismounted at the front of Carmody's saloon and slowly looped his buckskin's reins to a pole. Then the wagon was past and Brad saw the store clerk stand back to throw a glance at him. He shook his head after a moment and said something to the woman that was obviously in reply to a question. Then, in a raised voice: 'I see Mr Allison along the street yonder with Clete Baxter.'

'All right, Ike, all right. They can join when they wish.'

Brad was fingering for his tobacco sack when the batwing doors of Carmody's saloon were thrown open and a red-faced cowhand staggered on to the plank sidewalk. Sweat shone on the ruddy forehead, and the eyes had a drunken, heedless roll to them. The waddy had a six-shooter in his right hand, and Brad ducked hastily as it was swept up in reckless fashion and a bullet was blasted at the blue-vaulted sky.

'Hell and damnation!' Brad roared. 'You crazy son ...'

Instinctively, his right fist shot out and

9

cracked solidly on the angle of the cowboy's jaw, flinging him into an awkward spin. On the same instant a shrill whistling of horses and stamping of hooves brought Brad pivoting to look where the spooked wagon team was bucking and threshing in the shafts.

The woman with the corn-coloured hair sawed desperately at the ribbons, calling and coaxing, but the horses had snatched the bits in their teeth and, with a loud whinnying, they tore into the middle of the road and began a mad race down the street.

A couple of men on foot tried to get out of the path of the runaways, and were bowled into the dust, yelping, and scrabbling for safety. Others on the sidewalks cried out and pointed, and Brad saw a stockily-built man who could have been in his fifties and who was already quite grey, bellow and rush out in front of the team, waving his arms and shouting.

'Clete, do something,' the grey-haired

man cried. 'Stop them! Glory, drag down hard, woman. Keep your nerve. Hang on ...'

The cowman was obliged to leap aside at the last instant, and the horses continued their frantic gallop, rounding a corner and vanishing from view in a high cloud of lemon-tinted dust.

Brad dashed to his buckskin and flipped the reins free. With a leap he was astride while the horse was already on the move. Yells of encouragement rang out, and the elderly cowman shouted something at him as he tore past.

Around the corner, Brad glimpsed the wagon careering towards the outskirts of the town, the woman still aboard, her hat lost and her hair flying in the wind. He raked the buckskin's flanks with his heels, speaking throatily as he lay forward, head low. Now they were in the open, with the yellow trail-dust flashing past in a sun-dappled pattern. On their right was the spur-line station with its loading pens;

on the left the silver ribbon of river that furnished the town's water supply.

Brad knew that he was gaining on the runaways, and he marvelled at the woman's grit for hanging on. A weaker member of her sex might have let go of the traces, might even have fainted and been thrown to the ground. He called to her as he drew level and caught a glimpse of wide eyes where hope speedily supplanted fear and shock. She screamed some answer that was shredded on the wind, but Brad paid no heed, fighting the bucking into line with the trumpeting off-side horse.

He paused for a second to catch his breath and judge timing and distance. Then, poising in the stirrups, he lunged out, and for a sickening space was suspended in mid-air with the wind and dust whistling about him. His fingers sought and found purchase. He grabbed madly as the leathers skidded through his fingers. Then he had a grip and was bucking on his mount's back, tugging and rasping, and finally slewing the runaways into a close, grinding circle that sent the wagon crashing against the unyielding trunk of a massive oak.

The shock effectively halted the team horses, and they pawed and neighed, giving Brad time to jump to the ground and make the ribbons secure to a wheel spoke. Now he turned his attention to the woman, seeing a face that was pale as death. Her eyelids fluttered, and he feared she would topple from the seat. Instead, she dropped into his arms, her breath beating warmly against his cheek, her trembling bosom close to his chest, her large eyes staring at him.

'Thank you,' she whispered after a moment. 'Oh, thank you. Would you— would you let me down?'

'Sure thing, ma'am.'

His initial impulse was to hold on to her for as long as he might, but he lowered her gently to the ground and bent over her. He remembered the canteen on the buckskin and hastened to get it, uncorking it swiftly and holding it to her lips. She took a short drink and some colour returned to her cheeks.

'It needed a—real man to do that,' she breathed. 'I might have been killed, and then Hank would have had the laugh ...'

Brad frowned, wondering if the shock had affected her mind in some queer fashion. 'Guess I don't follow you, ma'am,' he said. 'And don't make a fuss about it. Anybody could have done what I did. It was the drunk firing his gun who made the horses spook ... Say, here's more menfolk arriving.'

It was true. A half-dozen galloping riders were strung out in the roadway, their horses' hooves kicking up fountains of dust. Brad soon recognized the stocky, middle-aged man. A tall, muscularly-built rider raced along at his side. They churned off the road and dragged their horses to a standstill, scrambling to the ground and rushing towards Brad and the woman.

'Glory, honey, are you all right?'

Brad stood back while the grey-haired cowman bent beside her, concern cutting deep grooves into his leathery face. The second arrival seemed equally agitated and stooped to take Glory Allison's hand. In that brief instant Brad's sharp mind was able to assess a couple of points that caused his brows to arch.

'How do you feel, Glory?'

'Just a bit shaken, I guess, Clete,' she responded. 'If I could get to my feet ...'

The other would-be rescuers had clattered up to the scene, but they remained in their saddles when they saw that the situation was well in hand.

'Your wife all right, Hank?' a skinny townsman inquired.

'Guess so, Fox,' the cowman replied. 'But if it hadn't been for this stranger there's no telling what might have happened. I'm beholden to you, mister,' he added.

'Forget it.' Brad was mildly surprised

at the difference in ages between the man and his wife. But where did the dark-featured, handsome Clete fit into the picture? Brother? Hank Allison's ramrod? Clete was certainly evincing more than brotherly concern as he held on to Glory's arm.

Suddenly Clete turned to the team horses, anger leaping into his eyes. 'These damn nags are responsible for everything,' he grated. 'They need a lesson.'

Brad watched narrowly as he picked a short-handled whip from the well of the wagon and shook out the lash. He stepped to the still-trembling horses and smote the nearest one across the face, making it whistle and stamp.

'Hold on!' Brad shouted. 'No call for that.'

Clete Baxter glared at him, pulling his underlip between his teeth. 'You've done your bit, mister,' he said meagrely. 'And we're thanking you. But you'd better go about your business.'

'Well, your gratitude is well taken, friend,' Brad told him while he let his gaze absorb the other. 'But you can't just take to whipping the horses. It wasn't their fault in the first place.'

'He's right, Clete,' someone chipped in. 'It was a cowpoke—Luke Greer, I think. He was drunk as usual, and fired his gun into the air.'

'No matter,' Clete said doggedly. 'These lunkheads need a lesson.'

He was raising the whip again when Brad spoke once more, only now his tone was edged with steel.

'You beef the horses, mister, and I reckon I'll have to beef you.'

'Say, what the blazes ...'

Baxter simply stared for a moment, scarcely able to believe what he had just heard. Then he bellowed a hard laugh and took a couple of paces towards the tall, lean-bodied man who was standing with legs slightly apart and thumbs hooked into his shell-belt.

'Do you know who you're talking to, pilgrim?' he demanded brusquely.

'I know *what* I'm talking to,' Brad replied. 'And what I said goes, no matter what label you carry on your coat. So don't whip that nag again, friend.'

'By grab! Of all the nervy characters I've ever come across ...'

'Clete,' the woman broke in quickly. 'Call it off. There really is no need to beat the dumb animals.' Her eyes sought the stranger's uncompromising gaze as she spoke, but Brad continued to regard the handsome Baxter to the exclusion of everything else. He believed he had judged correctly in assuming that he was Hank Allison's foreman.

'Sure,' Allison butted in with a shake of his head. 'Let it ride, Clete.' He moved to Brad and stuck his hand out. 'Name's Hank Allison, mister. I'm in your debt, and don't you forget it. Remember, too, that I'm a man of my word.'

'Wouldn't argue with you on that score,

Mr Allison,' the tall man drawled. 'But you're over-rating what I did. Anyway, my handle is Brad Travis.'

Allison beamed at him. 'Cowhand, by the looks of you?'

'Cowhand is right, sir,' Brad smiled. 'Some of the time anyhow.'

'Meaning you're out of a job at the minute?'

'Well, I—uh—Look, Mr Allison, that doesn't matter right now. I wouldn't want to trade on your good nature.'

'Well said, mister,' Clete Baxter chipped in patronisingly. He had managed to drag up a weak smile from somewhere. He offered his hand to the stranger. 'I like a man who can stand on his own feet and who doesn't go around hunting for hand-outs. No hard feelings, I hope?'

'I'm not a spiteful man, Baxter.'

Brad allowed his fingers to touch the foreman's. His obvious reluctance to shake with the handsome man produced a tide of dark colour. But it was evident that

Clete was schooled in the art of hiding his feelings. He merely grinned sheepishly. Then he became businesslike and gave his attention to Glory Allison.

'You ride my horse back home, and I'll handle the wagon,' he told her. 'No telling when the nags'll take it into their heads to act up again.'

Brad went to the buckskin and levered himself aboard. He turned back towards the main street of the town, patting his mount's neck as he went. 'Sorry to have been so rough with you, pard. But we just had to save that lady's neck.'

As for the rancher, Hank Allison he didn't realize that the stranger had left them until he heard the steady clip-clopping of hooves. Then he shouted something and Brad twisted in his saddle and threw a salute. He hadn't gone far when a couple of the townsmen on horses caught up. They were open and friendly, and talked of the swift manner in which he had gone after the wagon with the spooked team.

'Hank won't forget it, mister,' one of them declared. 'He's got his heart in the right place. And if you happen to be looking for a job you needn't look much further.'

'Good cow country then?'

'Certainly is for the right sort of rider. But there's plenty of roughnecks and hell-raisers, just like everywhere else. That Luke Greer's one of them. If Luke has any sense he'll keep out of Clete Baxter's way for a spell. Clete's dangerous when he's roused.'

'He really is Allison's foreman?'

'Sure thing. Good man with men and cattle.'

'With women too, you bet!' the other townsman interjected with a chuckle. 'And Hank must be blind if he can't see—'

'Easy on the gossip,' the first speaker admonished, tipping his companion a wink that Brad was not supposed to see.

Well, he was a stranger to this burg, Brad decided whimsically, and he must find out things for himself. But he got the implication all the same. The good-looking Clete Baxter had his hat tipped at Hank Allison's young wife. The knowledge irked Brad, but then he told himself that it was none of his affair. If a middle-aged cowman wanted to marry a girl much younger than himself, it was surely the exclusive business of the parties concerned.

Brad was glad when they reached the heart of the town. He was growing tired of the chatter of the two men who had chosen to accompany him. Their talk was superficial and innocuous now, to do with the range surrounding the town of Oxbow and the bother that some of the ranchers were having with rustlers. Then the pair decided they had gone far enough with him, and the first speaker saw fit to remind Brad that he could do worse than sign on with Hank Allison's outfit.

Brad said thanks and so long. Instead of stopping at Carmody's saloon again, he rode on along the rutted road until he came to the livery stable and barn. He rode inside and booked a stall and a feed of grain for the buckskin.

He paid rent for a day, not at all sure of how long he might stay in town. Then he headed back to the saloon and ordered a beer. It was cool and bitter, and it helped to clear a lot of trail-dust from his throat.

He was on his second drink when the stout bartender leaned over the counter and spoke in an undertone. 'You're the gent that swiped Luke Greer with a handful of knuckles when he spooked the Allison horses?'

'That's true,' Brad agreed. 'So what?'

'Oh, nothing much maybe. Just a tip, mister. Luke's a mighty proddy cuss, and he's bragging about what he's going to do to you.'

Brad's grin was easy and tolerant. 'I won't be far away for the next hour or so. In fact, I'm taking this beer to yon table to rest my weary legs. You don't have any objections?'

'You're welcome, stranger.' The bartender accompanied that with a closer, more penetrating look at the newcomer.

Brad had just begun to relax, and was in the process of twisting up a quirly when the batwing doors were thrust open and the red-faced cowhand called Luke Greer elbowed in from the sunlight.

Two

The waddy took a couple of lurching steps across the floor and addressed the bartender.

'Phil, have you seen any sign of that ranny yet? Hear he come back into town again ...'

'I'm right here 'poke,' Brad called to him. He watched the way the cowboy turned about, at the same time making a clumsy effort to get his revolver clear of its holster. Brad added with a sharpness to his voice while he let the muzzle of his own Colt .45 show above the edge of the table: 'Don't do anything you mightn't live to regret, sonny.'

The cool, deliberate warning put Greer to rocking up on his boot-heels while his fingers held his revolver frozen in a half-draw. He pulled a hard breath to his lungs and growled: 'You damn upstart! Who in hell do you think you are? Why did you pick on me, mister?'

'Never picked on anybody,' Brad responded flatly. 'But you must have a bad memory if you can't recall scattering Hank Allison's horses. His wife might have been killed. Why not sober up and hit the trail home?'

Greer laughed at that, finding some joke lurking in the stranger's advice. His hand came away from his gun and he crossed to the table where Brad sat. There, he proceeded to place a friendly arm about the tall man's shoulder.

'Know something, mister? I reckon I like you, for all your cussed uppishness. That was a real snifter you caught me. Say, what about putting that hogleg back where it belongs and let's have a little drink together? What about it? Let bygones be bygones, like the preacher said. What about it?'

'Suits me.'

Brad pouched his gun as he spoke. He wasn't fast enough to trap Greer's hand before it had grabbed his beer glass and cracked the rim against the edge of the table. The jagged remains were thrust to within a couple of inches of Brad's face.

'Don't move, sonny,' the cowhand hissed while a triumphant laugh bubbled in his throat. 'You figured you'd picked on some soft mark, didn't you? Well, now you see how you were badly mistook. Luke Greer don't take dirt from nobody.'

'You're crazy,' Brad said from dry lips.

'Yeah? Well, you could be right, mister. I should have figured that out for myself. Oh, I'm crazy right enough! Crazy smart, boy, and a mite too slick for a drifter like you. Know what I'm gonna do to your purty dial?'

The bartender was on the verge of despair. His face ran with sweat; his eyes rolled; he was pulling at his hands in a paroxysm of fear. 'Ease up. Luke,' he pleaded. 'Do you want to get yourself put behind bars? Maybe for a long time, Luke?'

'Stay out of this, Phil,' Greer told him. 'You're a good Injun, but you sure as hell talk too much.'

The torn edge of the glass jerked closer until a sharp point touched Brad's left cheek. He felt the prick and drew back a little. A tiny dribble of blood ran down to his chin. Greer howled with laughter.

'G'wan!' he taunted. 'you're purty white around the gills about now, mister. You look like you might start crying any minute. Say, you're whiter'n a ghost, nearly. But I'll soon colour you up ...'

Brad had been working his fingers carefully towards his bolstered Colt. Now his hand closed on the butt of the weapon. He withdrew it slowly, eased back the hammer with the utmost caution. His eyes never left the cowboy's face. He judged that if he shot him from under the table, the bullet would take him somewhere in the legs.

'Luke, why don't you do what the barkeep says? let up. Forget it. Don't do something you'll regret.'

'I'm going to make you say you're sorry for hitting me, boy,' the other gloated. 'You do that real quick and I mightn't cut you so bad. Say "I'm sorry, Uncle Luke." Come on, say it!'

Brad was on the point of squeezing trigger when the saloons doors swung open and he glimpsed the rancher Hank Allison come in, his foreman at his back.

A single glance told the cowman what was going on, and he lost no time in hauling his revolver out. He practically screamed at Greer.

'Drop that glass quick as blazes, Luke, or I'll put daylight through your miserable guts.'

The cowhand moved his head, and that was the moment Brad chose to bury his left fist into his stomach. Back the tormentor went, the broken glass sailing from his fingers. He struck the floor and rolled, groaning and retching. He began to blubber something about ' ... didn't mean no harm ...'

'You dirty bastard, Luke,' Hank Allison yelled.

'Was only a joke, Mr Allison. Just a—joke.'

'I suppose that's what you call scaring Mrs Allison's team?' Clete Baxter flung at him, deciding to take a hand in the game.

He reached Greer as the cowhand made it to his knees, and grabbed a handful of his shirt-front. Baxter pulled him closer and raked his face viciously with his bunched knuckles, swearing softly all the while. Then his fist shot out and landed on the tip of Greer's chin, flinging him against the bar. The cowhand tried to claw at the edge of the counter for support, missed his grip, and slumped to his knees.

'Let him be, Clete,' Hank Allison grated. 'He's as drunk as all get-out. He doesn't know what he's doing.'

'He knows well enough, Boss.' Baxter kicked Greer soundly in the ribs, eliciting a sharp cry of pain. And when the luckless cowboy tried to protect himself he was kicked on the other side of his chest. He screeched in agony and flopped down on his face.

'That'll do,' Brad snapped. 'I could have handled him well enough myself.'

'Yes, so I noticed,' the foreman said scathingly. 'If we hadn't come in when we did he'd likely have cut you into ribbons about an inch wide. Anyhow, you helped us when we were in trouble, and now we've helped you. Looks like we can call it quits.'

'Ain't the way you figure, Clete,' the bartender interposed. 'The stranger's right when he says he could have handled Luke. He had his gun out, and I reckon Luke was about to get a bad pain in the legs when you folks arrived.'

Baxter and the bartender lifted Luke Greer from the floor and hauled him unceremoniously to the batwing doors. The bartender had the presence of mind to relieve Greer of his gun before they dumped him on the sidewalk. Back in the saloon, Clete Baxter wiped his hands as if they had been badly fouled and looked at the Colt which was now being stored at the back of the counter.

'Don't let him get it, Phil. I'll make a complaint to Sheriff Adrian and see if he can't keep that ranny off the streets when he's on a drunk.'

'They say he's decent enough when he's sober,' the bartender said. 'He'd give a pard the last cent he had.'

'Trouble would be getting him when he is sober,' Baxter grunted. He accepted the bottle that was pushed across to him and poured into two glasses, signalling for Hank Allison to join him. The rancher shook his head and then Baxter glanced at Brad. 'Want a snort to settle you?'

'No, thanks.'

Brad's refusal didn't go down well with

the foreman, and after swallowing his drink he swung to the saloon doors. 'If you're set on that notion of yours, I'll leave you to it, Hank,' he informed his boss airily over his shoulder. 'But, like I warned you, you should make sure what it is you're buying. You could find yourself on the wrong end of a bad deal.'

'I know what I'm doing, Clete,' the rancher responded with a touch of irritation in his voice. 'Say,' he added when the thought occurred to him, 'why don't you and Glory head on home? I'll be along afterwards.'

Brad was quick to notice the glint that betrayed itself momentarily in the foreman's eye. But Baxter soon caught himself and shrugged, making an elaborate show of indifference.

'Whatever you say. That scare shook her up a bit.'

'Yeah, I know. Go ahead then, Clete.'

Brad watched as Baxter continued to the doorway and thrust through with a movement of shoulders that amply illustrated his vanity and arrogance. He stifled a plucking of annoyance as the rancher nodded towards a table. He was smiling broadly now, back in control of himself.

'Can we set and talk for a minute, mister?' he asked Brad.

'Why not?'

How dumb could a man get, Brad reflected then; how blind could a man become, not being able to tell the difference between a friend and an enemy? It was obvious to anyone with his wits about him that Clete Baxter had his eye on Allison's good-looking wife. Indeed, their relationship might already have reached the stage where the woman preferred Baxter's charms to those of her husband. But the rancher might know all about that and had said to himself 'what the hell' and looked the other way.

Sitting opposite Allison, with another schooner of beer in front of him, Brad discarded that last notion. Hank Allison could not be called old, by any stretch of the imagination. He was short and heavily-built, and exuded strength and vitality. His eyes held a cheerful sparkle now as they rested on the stranger, and something Glory had said returned to Brad. *'I might have been killed, and then Hank would have had the laugh ...'*

He realized that the cowman was talking to him.

'In spite of the impression Clete might have given you, Travis, I'd like to hire you for purely selfish reasons. I could use a man of your—uh—capabilities. Do you get that straight enough?'

Brad grinned at him. Quite apart from his earlier reservations about having anything more to do with the Allison outfit, he found himself liking the man seated in front of him. There was a blunt honesty in the way he spoke that was refreshing and infectious.

'Sure, I get it, Mr Allison. But there's

bound to be a lot of capable rannies roaming around who'd jump at the chance of a job with you.'

'Maybe so.' Allison took a sip of whisky. 'But I don't think many of them would measure up to your calibre. You've shown you know how to act in an emergency. You've shown you have the sort of nerve that I like in a man ...'

Allison let his words trickle away, smiling wryly at some secret thought. He asked the bartender to fetch a couple of cigars, and when he had applied a match to Brad's before lighting his own, he sighed heavily and some of the warmth melted out of his face.

'Would you mind if I took you into my confidence. Travis? I can call you Brad, I guess?'

'That's my handle.'

At this juncture something told Brad to make an excuse and leave Allison on his own. He had the feeling that the rancher was about to make some disclosure concerning his wife. He wanted no part in domestic squabbles or differences of opinion. Glory Allison was a young and desirable woman, and that was that. If she preferred the arms of a man closer to her own age, then it was Allison's fault for being foolish enough to marry her in the first place. Again, if Clete Baxter was shallow enough and weak enough to yield to temptation, why didn't the rancher take the easy way out and get rid of him?

'Can we talk straight, Travis?'

'If you want to. But we'd better get one thing straight, Mr Allison: I'm just a drifter, as you can see. You know nothing about my past or my background, and it would be a mistake to risk—'

Allison's upraised hand stopped him. 'Are you suggesting I can't see what's in front of me?' he queried softly. 'I can read a man, Travis. You strike me as honest and trustworthy. In this country it's all the bill of sale a *hombre* needs. Now listen ... I run a pretty sizable ranch out at Spanish Flat. The Flat has some of the richest grazing land in these parts. I run a herd that's second to none in size and quality. I keep a dozen riders the year round. Maybe you think that makes me a generous fool, but you'd be wrong. I've good reason for running a decent-sized crew.'

Brad smiled thinly. 'The best reason in the world, I bet. Rustlers?'

'Then you've heard what's happening here?'

Brad shrugged. He puffed at his cigar, deciding that, all in all, he wasn't doing so badly for a drifter who had been smitten with the idea of seeing the other side of a tall hill. Still, it could be that things were going just too well. There could be a snag that it would pay him to look for now instead of stumbling on later.

'I heard someone say that cattle thieves are pretty busy in this neck of the woods,' he conceded. 'But you'll always get the widelooper where there's cows. What kind of law have you hereabouts?'

It was Hank Allison's turn now to look speculative and twitch his shoulders. 'Ben Adrian's a good man,' he said slowly, picking his words. 'Solid, but a mite slow. But Ben and his deputy, Lem Farmer, do their best. They managed to catch three rustlers this month, had them tried and shipped off to four years apiece in the pen. But that's just skimming the surface. It's the working cowboy who's your best bet against these rogues. But I reckon you know that already?'

'I know.'

So far, nothing the rancher had told him had anything to do with underlying worries or fears, and Brad found a little of the tension easing out of him. He liked playing his game out in the open, where there could be no room for accusations of subterfuge or mischief-making should the whole business finish in a showdown.

Allison was casting an appraising eye over the big room. There were about a dozen customers in evidence, mostly locals.

The rancher said suddenly: 'Do you want a job, Travis?'

'That's sure handsome of you, Mr Allison. Could I think about it?'

'Why not? Needing time to study a situation falls in with your character. But I want you to give me your answer by morning. A straight yes or a straight no. My outfit is the Bar A. That suit you?'

'Suits me fine, sir. And thanks.'

'My pleasure.' Allison prepared to rise, then paused as if debating something with himself. The gaze he bent on the younger man was level and candid.

'Something bothering you?' Brad nudged when he seemed undecided.

'I reckon. There's something else I think you ought to know, Brad. And I guess I'd better admit it's the real reason I want to hire someone like you. You—you won't say I'm crazy?'

'Not until I hear what's on your mind.'

Brad forced a faint smile, but he soon sobered. 'Shoot.'

'Somebody is after my scalp.'

Brad almost laughed in his face, but there was something pathetically sincere about the way the confession was made. He was aware of a little tingle running along his spine. There was no doubt that Hank Allison seemed a worried man just then. He looked hounded, haunted. He was roaming around in some dark valley that could well be of his own making.

Brad lifted his shoulders and spread his hands. 'Well, just think about it,' he said, trying to sound easy. 'You're a big operator after all. You're bound to have made enemies as well as friends. There's nothing very strange in that.'

'You're just trying to humour me, Travis,' the cowman retorted. 'This is not a case of figuring I have to keep looking over my shoulder as I ride down the main street of Oxbow, or that I imagine there's a mad killer hiding behind every rock.'

'I see,' Brad murmured slowly. His cigar had gone out and he struck a match to light it. 'Really something definite? No bats flying around in your head? No nightmares that don't stay behind when you get out of bed?'

'Nothing like that, I tell you. It's this one man. A bushwhacker.'

Brad emitted a low whistle. Allison had sunk back down on to his chair. He finished the dregs of his whisky at a gulp.

'Tell me about it.'

'I've told you. A bushwhacker. He has made three tries to bring me down. Missed three times.'

'Maybe he intends to miss.'

'Don't you believe it! They were all long shots with a rifle. Maybe the next time he'll—'

'Does your foreman know about this?' Brad interrupted him. In spite of not wishing to become embroiled in Allison's problems, domestic or otherwise, he found himself becoming genuinely curious about what was going on.

'Sure, I've told Clete. He pretends to take me seriously, but I reckon he's just stringing me along and thinks I've got a bee in my hat.'

'He has no right to think that. What about your wife—how does she figure it?'

A quick change came into the rancher's face, and it was as though he had suddenly dropped a curtain. He realized that Brad was watching him closely and stammered: 'I—I haven't told Glory about it. I've warned Clete against telling her. I don't want to worry her, Travis. She's the dearest thing I have. You've seen what a beauty she is?'

The gleam in his eye caused a coldness to settle in the pit of Brad's stomach. But he drummed up a feeble grin, nodded.

'Anybody can see that, Mr Allison.'

'So you won't ever mention it to her?' He pulled a wry grin. 'I'm assuming that you'll come and work for me. I hope you will. A man like you could maybe get to the bottom of the deal—help root out the rustlers, and at the same time maybe find out who wants me dead, and why.'

Brad pulled a long breath to his lungs and expelled it slowly down his nostrils. His cigar had gone out again and he struck another match to light it. A worry was stirring at the back of his mind; his eyes narrowed as he framed a question.

'Why are you picking on me—a drifter who's just hit town and who could be gone again by dawn?'

'But I told you why. The way you handled that team ...'

'Rubbish,' Brad snapped, losing his patience. 'If you're going to play a square game we'd better get moving together in a straight line. I'm asking you—why me?'

Allison drew his lips away from his teeth momentarily in what looked like a pained grimace. He leaned across the table and spoke in a taut whisper. 'All right, mister. You've called my bluff. As soon as I heard your name mentioned something clicked. Know how it is? For a while I couldn't grab it, but then it really hit me.'

Brad was frowning darkly. He drew back a little, regarding the cowman through a cloud of smoke. 'What hit you?'

'Isabel,' Allison said with a quick glance over his shoulder.

'A woman or a town?' Brad's features were inscrutable.

'I don't know any woman called Isabel, friend. But I did hear of a town called Isabel. And a man who was known as Marshal Brad Travis. This fella Travis made four kinds of hell for a bunch of sidewinders who reckoned they'd come on an easy mark. You're the same Travis, aren't you?'

Brad shrugged, sighed, wished he was fifty miles away. 'I thought I'd left all that behind me,' he said after a moment's reflection. 'These days I find cowpunching a less onerous chore. But one thing, mister, you'll keep quiet about what you know?'

45

'It's a deal.' The rancher beamed suddenly, and it was as though a heavy weight had been removed from his shoulders. 'But remember,' he added in a sober voice, 'what one man can figure out, so can another.'

'I certainly hope not. But if that happens, Mr Allison, then I'm afraid I'll have to rattle my hocks pretty fast. I've got a couple of long shadows on my back-trail that would like to overtake me.'

They talked for another few minutes in more general terms, Allison giving the newcomer a quick run-down on the situation in the territory. There was no more mention of Glory, and for that at least Brad was grateful. But he was puzzled all the same, and irritated by some niggling doubt that insisted on hiding itself at the back of his mind.

Finally, Hank Allison put his proposition to the younger man with renewed urgency.

'We'll talk tactics later. I'm not trying to buy your gun, you must remember. I need your nerve and your know-how. How about it, Brad?'

'I don't see much reason why I shouldn't give it a whirl,' Brad decided at length. 'Tell me how to get to your place?'

'Come with me now and you'll see the way,' the other invited.

But Brad shook his head. 'Let it sit until morning.'

And so it came about that, a short time later, Hank Allison left him to his own devices. Brad soon became aware of several men regarding him surreptitiously, and after a while he moved over to the counter and ordered a whisky—something he rarely if ever indulged in.

Three

Spanish Flat turned out to be everything Hank Allison said it was. The grassy plains stretched, apparently to infinity, lush and well-watered, a veritable cattleman's paradise. To the east, and piled on the horizon-line like small sandhills, were blue-tinted mountains. A week's journey, Brad calculated. The south and west had scatterings of timber, gentle hills where deer would roam in profusion, and where there surely must be cold, blue pools running with rainbow trout.

To the north, the grass rolled out like the waves of an ocean, smoky and dreamy under this benign sunlight. Cattle ranged everywhere, and only when Brad stared long enough and hard enough did he make out the dim shapes of riders.

But no sooner had he entered this vast domain than he felt he was being watched. At first the notion irked him when he could see nothing to substantiate the suspicion, but then he realized that Allison would have to exercise supreme caution and wariness. The need seemed totally out of keeping with the surroundings. Why should men stalk this bounteous land with roguery in their hearts? Why should anyone harbour thoughts of murder when the very air breathed of charity and peace?

Ancient memories began to thrum to the surface of Brad's consciousness, and became part of the events of yesterday. Perhaps he was a fool after all to have anything to do with Spanish Flat and Allison's Bar A ranch. That woman was trouble, for a start, and Clete Baxter had the makings of a dangerous enemy. It all made a pretty picture—rustlers, a bushwhacker, and a beautiful woman framed in the centre of things!

'A hell's brew, if ever there was one.'

Still, the whole set-up was highly intriguing and not without the savour of challenge. In such circumstances, it was difficult for Brad to remind himself that he had vowed never to meet trouble head-on again as long as he lived.

Finally, he saw the ranch headquarters sitting squarely on a wide bench where oaks and cottonwoods predominated, a substantial scattering of buildings that were well cared for and which surely represented the acme of any cattleman's ambition.

He was drawing closer to the fenced front yard with its massive hanging Bar A emblem when a horseman appeared suddenly, riding in on his right. The man merely glanced at the newcomer before continuing to the rear of the lay-out, but Brad knew with a throbbing certainty that this was the rider who had shadowed him every mile of the way since his buckskin set its first hoof on Bar A grass.

Brad went on through the gateway and halted before a long, railed porch where a rocker moved gently as if someone had lately risen from it. He brought his mount to the drinking-trough, and was wiping the sweatband of his hat when someone called from the porch.

'Mr Travis!'

He jerked around quickly—too quickly, he told himself—and touched the brim of the hat he had replaced on his head. Nevertheless, he could not smother the faint smile of pleasure that creased the corners of his mouth.

'Good morning, Mrs Allison. Is the boss around?'

'He's out and about somewhere,' Glory Allison explained. 'But he shouldn't be long. Turn your horse out and then come up here.'

'Thank you, ma'am.'

She was like a prairie flower that you just wanted to stand and look at. And even from this distance she had the power to send a wild tingle dancing along his spine.

Brad slipped the bit and loosened the cinch. He stood by the horse until it had finished drinking. He slapped its nose fondly. He knew the woman was still standing there, still watching his every move. What did she think of him? What did she expect of him? Of course she would not know of her husband's worries, and of Allison's reason for asking him to sign on the Bar A payroll. Or would she? Brad had the notion that Glory might know a lot more than Hank figured.

He took the horse to the back and asked a grizzled oldster emerging from the barn which corral he might use. A finger pointed while the old fellow shifted a tobacco chew from one cheek to the other.

'You can stow your gear in the barn if you're staying a while.'

'Thanks.'

Brad opened the corral gate and turned the buckskin loose with a dozen frisky-looking beasts. He dallied for the time it took to fashion a cigarette, then shouldered his saddle and gear and cut over to the barn.

In the pool of shadow just inside the doorway he halted abruptly to squint at a lanky cowhand squatting on an upturned box.

The waddy nodded casually. 'Howdy, stranger.' He was youngish, fresh-faced, with bold eyes and an easy manner. He was the sort that would not be easily flustered.

'Howdy yourself,' Brad grunted, finding a nail and tacking a stirrup over it. 'Nice outfit you've got here,' he added conversationally.

'Reckon it'll do till something better turns up.' A ready grin robbed the observation of guile. 'Are you the new man the boss is supposed to have took on?'

'That could be me, I reckon. Name of Travis.'

'I'm Jack Mitchell. Pleased to meet you, Travis.' He heaved himself to his feet and extended a hand that Brad readily grasped.

'Fact is, we could do with a couple of extra men about now. But I guess you know all about that?'

Brad took the bait. He nodded, sobering. 'Rustlers?'

'And then some! No matter how hard we watch, they always find a loophole to worm some beeves through. Man would think they had good friends at this outfit.' He laughed. 'Don't take that too seriously though. I watched you come across the Flat. Know I was trailing you?'

'Let's say I felt your beady eyes on the back of my head. But you don't have to take that too seriously either. Well, I'd better pad on round to the house and pay my respects.'

'Sure thing. Pleased to meet you, fella. And good hunting.'

Brad couldn't quite decide whether a double meaning was intended. He had been on his way to the open, but he wheeled and studied Jack Mitchell for a moment. The cowhand was smiling ingenuously at him, and he shrugged and left him.

Glory Allison was still on the porch when he arrived at the front once more. This morning she wore a riding skirt and white blouse, open at the neck. Her mass of golden hair was bunched and trapped with a piece of yellow ribbon. She smiled and rose from the rocker as he climbed the four steps. She held out a slim-fingered hand that was soft and surprisingly cool to the touch.

'I'll take this opportunity to thank you again for everything you did yesterday, Mr Travis.'

'Forget it, Mrs Allison. It was no more than any man would have done.'

'But you were the only one alert enough and daring enough to take your horse and come after the team,' she insisted in a voice that had gone husky.

Brad was finding this meeting intensely embarrassing; privately, he questioned her sincerity. Glory Allison was obviously a

56

woman well used to twining men around her little finger. She expected him to blush like a kid having praise heaped on him, and she was not disappointed. Brad cursed himself for his weakness, vowing that he would give her no other chance to manoeuvre him into a similar situation.

'Come inside and wait for Hank,' she invited. 'He rode out a short time ago with Clete Baxter. But, as I said, he shouldn't be long.'

'I could wait just as well in the bunkhouse, ma'am.'

'Of course you won't! By tomorrow you might be one of the hired hands, but for the moment you're a guest and shall be treated as such.'

'If you insist,' he said, pulling his hat through his fingers.

'I surely do, sir!'

She led him into a parlour that was simply but adequately furnished, and assigned him a chair that afforded a view of the front yard and the whole green sweep of Spanish Flat stretching off to the south.

She indicated a cabinet with a couple of bottles and glasses ranged on top. 'A drink?'

'No, thank you. I don—'

'Aw, come on! Just a spot of prime bourbon to wash the dust out of your tonsils? Isn't that a favourite cowboy saying?'

Brad shrugged and yielded for the sake of courtesy. She laughed at his expression, a low, tinkling sound that might easily have been interpreted as bold and provocative. He took the glass she proffered and watched how she poured a generous splash for herself.

'Water?' she challenged suddenly, and Brad reluctantly refused.

She took a chair opposite him. 'You mustn't think that I make a habit of drinking, Mr Travis. Look, would you mind if I called you Brad? It's your name, isn't it? And it's much easier to say.'

'Why not, ma'am?'

'And couldn't you manage Glory? That is, when we're together, of course.'

Brad felt heat pushing into his face, but this time he managed to control himself. He was finding out all too quickly the type of woman he might have to deal with.

'If you say so—uh—Glory.'

'That's better! And Brad, it really sounds something when you say my name that way. My real name was Gloriana, you know. Just imagine!' Her eyes twinkled into his and she extended her glass, clinking it gently against his own. 'To your future at Bar A, Brad.'

'To your good health, ma'am,' Brad responded evenly. 'And may you never have another scare like the one you had yesterday.'

'Heaven forbid!' She sipped and placed her glass on the table by the bottle. She stood up and put her back to him with a little flounce of her skirt, ostensibly to look through the window.

Brad stared hard at the trim back and the firm mould of hip and shoulder, his throat tightening in spite of the whisky he had swallowed. She whirled again quickly, surprising the calculating glint in his eye, smiling her appreciation of his reaction.

'Perhaps I should confess something, Brad: I've been wondering why Hank asked you to ride for him.'

His brain began working furiously now, sensing a trap of some kind that he must not fall into. Was it not enough for her that her husband wanted to hire an extra man who could prove useful to him?

'As a matter of fact I'm wondering something of the sort myself,' he said with a chuckle. 'I'm only a drifter after all, the kind that comes a dollar a dozen. But I guess your husband is grateful because I went to your help. He feels he owes me something.'

'But you *do* need a job, don't you?'

'I need a job right enough. And judging from what I've seen of this ranch, I'd say that any cowhand would forego a month's pay to get a berth here.'

'But you might be expected to do more than herd cattle to earn your pay,' she suggested soberly. 'Did Hank mention anything that might have led you to believe that?'

'He did mention rustlers.'

'Rustlers, yes! Rustlers seem to be everywhere these days. But cow-thieves are no strangers to cowboys.'

He evaded her direct gaze. 'That's true enough.'

'So perhaps Hank has some other reason for asking you to work for him? There might be some little special job he wishes you to attend to. Do you imagine so?'

It was difficult for him to meet her challenging stare while she said that. He cleared his throat, spoke huskily. 'If he has, ma'am, he hasn't mentioned it. And I can't think what other use I'd be to anybody apart from riding herd and maybe slinging a bullet at wideloopers.'

She moved over until she stood directly in front of him. If he stretched out a hand he could touch the tanned, velvet skin of her bare arm; a little higher and he might touch her face. This time he met the weight of her gaze without flinching, and now it was as if they were back on the main street of Oxbow again, discovering each other for the first time, appraising each other, exchanging subtle hints, challenges, promises. These were the sort of messages that required no words.

He was surprised when she said stiffly: 'Please get to your feet, Travis.'

'Sure thing, ma'am.'

He placed his glass on the table beside hers and rose. He towered almost a foot above her.

'Look at me, Brad,' she commanded.

'I'm looking, ma'am.' His tone was distant now, studiously cool.

'And stop calling me ma'am. I am not your ma'am, whatever that's supposed to mean.'

'What do I call you?' His voice had gone brittle.

'I want you to call me Glory.'

'But only when your husband isn't within earshot, huh?'

The impact of her right hand against his jaw produced a small explosion that rocked his head on his shoulders. The eyes that seared him were hot with anger. But there was something else there that Brad could not rightly fathom, even had he wanted to.

'You'd better not speak to me like that,' she breathed vibrantly. 'Don't dare say anything like that to me again.'

Brad shrugged. He started to smile, changed his mind, and shrugged once more. 'I reckon I just can't follow you, Glory,' he drawled. 'What did I do to win that slap?'

Whatever answer she might have vouch-safed was precluded by the sound of hoofbeats approaching the ranch buildings. There was more than one horse on the move. For an instant something akin to fear replaced the arrogance in the woman; then she had a grip on herself.

'Would you like to sit down again, Brad?' she said urgently. 'There must be other things we can discuss ...'

'No thanks, ma'am. If that's Mr Allison getting in, I'd better go and speak to him.'

'He'll see you here,' she insisted, not willing to surrender the initiative. 'Remember that for the time being you're still our guest.'

'I'll try to remember. Say ... do you mind if I have another snort of whisky to brace my nerve before your husband gets in?'

'Help yourself.'

He did so. It was a gesture, of course, designed to throw her off balance, if such a thing were possible. Glory Allison was a more complex creature than he had imagined. Cunning comprised a good deal of the mixture that formed her make-up.

She was dangerous as well, the way a keg of gun-powder was dangerous when some fool struck a match.

The hoofbeats hammered through the gateway and into the yard, and the horsemen ground their mounts to a halt amid much jingling of harness and whickering and whistling. Someone coughed to get rid of trail-dust, spat noisily. The rider spoke to his horse, saying something about 'you sassy old rebel'. A hard laugh followed, a gusty curse. Boots scraped up the steps to the porch and Glory moved out quickly to meet her husband.

'Your new rider got here all right, Hank.' She sounded like a little girl announcing something pleasant she had discovered.

'Well, that's something, by heaven ... Glory, know what? Another herd rustled out on the east corner. Fifty head or more ... Won't know until we run a proper tally.' The breath was hustling in his throat. 'The nerve of them! The damned gall ...'

'Easy, Hank,' his wife said in mollifying

fashion. 'Why don't you sit down and cool off? Hello, Clete. More trouble?'

Brad was on the porch by then, looking from one man to the other. Clete Baxter was dusty, his wind-blown features hot and glistening with perspiration. He climbed the four steps.

'You bet,' Clete said with feeling. All the while he had been observing the newcomer. 'Hello, Travis. So you got here right enough? Wondered if you'd come.' He turned to Allison, who by then was seated on the rocker, fanning himself with his hat-brim. 'Hank, maybe he's just what we need about now.' His eyes became bright, penetrating. 'Mister, have you ever handled a bunch of rustlers?'

Brad didn't miss the way the foreman's gaze leaped to Glory and then back to him, probing and suspicious.

'I've run across one or two in my time,' he replied evenly. 'Never heard of a simple way of dealing with them, though.'

'No? But maybe you know more than

you care to tell, mister?' Baxter's laugh was unpleasant, without humour. 'Hank, you old fox, I reckon I'm beginning to smell something. What am I missing?'

'Huh?' Glory had fetched two tall glasses of lemonade on a tray. She gave one to her husband, one to Baxter. Hank Allison took a long pull. He scowled at his foreman. 'What in hell are you driving at, Clete? You figure I'm holding a good hand of cards? You're a crazy son if you do.' He bestowed a twisted grin on Brad Travis. 'Say, big fella, squat here and listen to what's going on. This is part of your problem as well now. You ain't backing out?'

'I ain't backing out,' Brad replied. He realized that Allison was throwing dust over his tracks in case Clete Baxter discovered too much too soon. He squatted and looked across the yard. He could see a long way through the lemon sunlight from here. He could see cattle, the dim shapes of men. Closer up were the oak trees and cottonwoods. Clete Baxter was building a smoke. Allison asked his wife to fetch his pipe.

'Do you mind, honey?'

She smiled, stooped over him, and kissed him on the cheek. 'Don't move until you catch your breath. Another lemonade?'

'Thanks, honey.'

The lemonade came and the woman stayed. She put her back against the wall of the house where she could watch all three of them, listen to their talk. This was what might be termed a war party, planning how best to take the battle to the rustlers. Brad puffed at a cigarette and listened. One thing was certain: Clete Baxter knew what he was talking about, and he appeared to have the interests of the Bar A at heart. It was evident that Allison trusted him a lot.

When they had finished discussing how the rustlers had struck and where they might have taken the stolen stock, Hank Allison addressed himself to the new man, explaining the lay of the land, the tactics they had been using up to now. If the rancher was anxious to hear if Brad had any ideas, he refrained from asking in the foreman's presence.

Brad glanced across at Glory. She was looking out towards the range now, and it appeared to him that her thoughts were much further away than she could see ...

Four

He met the rest of the Bar A crew in the bunkhouse at sundown and thought the men were a pleasant enough bunch. Most of them had spent the day in trying to track down the rustlers who had been active the night before, and Hank Allison listened to their various reports with mounting impatience and frustration.

'Always just a handful of stuff,' he growled wrathfully. 'Big enough to make a handsome profit; small enough to get off the range quickly.'

'Enough to be herded by two or three men,' Brad interposed, and regretted speaking when all eyes immediately focused on him. Allison stared keenly at him for a moment while he appeared to assimilate what had just been said.

71

'By thunder, Travis, you could be right! A big gang would make a big cut when they're about it. Two or three men, as you say ... They would have to go slow and careful, and not be too greedy. Why in heck didn't I think of that angle before? Everybody expects these rogues to travel around in droves. But it mightn't be so.'

'Say, Boss, this fella Travis 'pears to have hit us like a gleam of light,' a redhead chuckled humourlessly.

Brad let his gaze drift to the speaker. Rusty Barnes was his name, and he puffed at a cigarette as he got out of his boots and spread his feet so that he might wiggle his toes.

'Doesn't take a lot of brains to figure that one, Rusty,' Brad observed.

'Course it don't.' Barnes winked at a friend. 'But you were the one who done it, mister. Makes the rest of us look like a pack of lunkheads.'

An anonymous giggle pushed colour through Brad's face and caused Hank

Allison to glower like a bear with a thorn in its paw.

'It's no damn laughing matter,' Allison snapped. 'And Travis really has shown me something I mightn't have thought of. Maybe two—three wideloopers? Even one maybe, with more brass than we expect? Can you beat it?'

'Aw, hell, Boss, give him a medal and let's get it over with,' another disgruntled cowboy snorted. 'What are you trying to tell us—that we're dumb? That we ain't pulling our weight?'

'That'll do, Wash,' a new voice chipped in from the bunkhouse doorway, and Brad looked to where Clete Baxter had just stepped through. 'Nobody's saying you're not pulling your weight, but we're losing stock and we'll have to catch the thieves.'

'Amen!' Rusty Barnes grunted.

Brad wasn't prepared for Baxter crossing the floor in two rapid strides and grabbing a handful of the redhead's shirtfront. He levered the puncher to his feet and glared at him. 'Quit trying to be funny.'

'All right, Clete, so it ain't funny. Did you hear anybody laughing?'

'Button your lip, Rusty, or I'll do it for you *pronto.*'

Brad watched the scene intently. He expected Barnes to make some other retort that would inflame the foreman further. Instead, the cowboy merely shrugged and brushed Baxter's hand away.

'Simmer down, Clete ... I'm sorry, Boss.'

'It's all right, Rusty.' Allison thrust his fingers through his thinning grey hair. 'Boys, I'm sorry if you think I've been riding you too hard. It's just that—well, hell, I'm kind of edgy.'

'Ain't we all?' someone else contributed sourly. 'But one of these days we'll latch on to these rogues, Boss; just wait and see.'

'One of these days!' Allison muttered under his breath and stormed outside.

When Clete Baxter had gone after him, Brad moved over to his bunk and spun up a cigarette. Five of the men congregated around the table in the middle of the floor and got a poker game going. Brad was invited to join in.

'I'm no great shucks at the pasteboards, boys.'

'Ain't that a surprise now?' Rusty Barnes drawled. 'Man would think you're a dab-shot at just about anything.'

'No need for that sort of talk,' Brad said quietly but firmly. 'If you want me to sit in, I will. I haven't got much *dinero* to lose though.'

'We'll be easy on you, pilgrim. Bring up a chair ... Look, you nosey gazebos,' Barnes said to the men who were watching, 'back off and write letters to your girls.' His remark seemed to remind him of something and he guffawed at the memory. 'Say, fellas, you know what? I done seen the lady of the house over at the creek with—' He broke off and coughed, glancing at Brad who had been watching him with brittle intensity. 'Well, never mind. A loose tongue never got a man very far.

Your deal, Perks, and watch them slick fingers of yours.'

'You mind your slick cracks,' Perks retorted airily. He licked a thumb before flipping the well-used cards to the players.

Brad was dealt a pair of tens, a king, a deuce and a four-spot. He discarded the deuce and four-spot and drew in another ten and a trey. The betting began. Perks and a stringy old-timer called Ward packed. Two of the others soon followed, and Barnes and Brad were left with a five-dollar pot between them. Barnes flung down three sevens with a five and an ace of spades, and swore when Brad displayed the tens.

'Curse you, mister,' he said without rancour. 'Figured you knew nothing about cards?'

'Not a lot, Rusty. But tens beats sevens, and I guess this is my five dollars.'

'I hate a bluffer like hell,' the redhead complained, temper edging into his tone. 'I surely do hate a bluffer.'

Brad subjected him to cool, unwavering regard. 'I think I'll drop out, if you don't mind, fella. A couple of games might take us into a row. You ought to play checkers yourself, Rusty. Easier on the nerves.'

'Why, you big-mouthed upstart ...'

Barnes' right fist was looping in towards Brad's head when Brad ducked and left the table in a quick, gliding movement and launched bunched knuckles at the other. The blow connected with Barnes' temple and sent him skidding to the floor.

'Don't try that with me, Rusty.'

'You dirty polecat!'

Brad's eye followed the frantic clawing of fingers for Barnes' gun. The redhead had the weapon half drawn when he found himself staring into the naked muzzle of the newcomer's .45.

'Don't try that trick either,' Brad whispered into the tense hush. He stood there, poised the way a hawk poises in the sky before striking, while the redhead's thoughts slithered around in a welter of indecision before settling craftily. A tremulous smile turned his mouth into a jagged gash.

'All right, pilgrim,' Barnes chuckled. 'Don't get your beard in a blaze on account of a small argument.'

'Don't buck me again like that, Rusty,' Brad warned him. 'Not unless you're willing to back your play to the hilt.' He pouched his revolver slowly and headed off to his bunk. He was angry with the cowhand, but a good deal angrier with himself. He had given Allison's cowboys an exhibition of his fast draw, and it was plain that all of them were impressed, even if not favourably so.

They would watch him more closely now, follow his movements, talk behind his back. He could almost hear the gist of their gossip: *'Hank Allison has hired a gunhand.'* It wouldn't matter how hard he tried to prove he was nothing more than a drifting cowpuncher. Nothing would change their minds about him, and from this moment on he needn't be surprised if he found himself left strictly alone, with no one he could depend on if he found himself in a tight spot.

Three weeks went past and Brad was still at the Bar A. He usually rode out at daybreak with the rest of the crew, performing the chores that a cowhand regarded as his lot in life and never to be taken too seriously. On several occasions Hank Allison took his new man to look at some location where he thought a rustler might be tempted to strike. Brad was asked for comments and advice which Allison imagined could be of some practical value.

'I'm no range-hawk,' Brad explained to the rancher at one point. 'And you mustn't think I am. Sure, I know cattle and I know plenty about men, but when your crew can't manage to get a lead on the rogues it's hardly likely that I can.'

'Don't get yourself into a sweat,' the

older man responded with a grin. 'Just keep your eyes and your ears open. Your training and experience are bound to mean something. And, Travis, when you do have an item of interest, come straight to me, will you?'

'Of course I will.'

Once again Brad sensed some underlying meaning in Allison's mode of talking. It was as though he wished to hint at something he was reluctant to come straight out with. What could it be—a possible association between his wife and the foreman? Did he have some inkling regarding the identity of the man he claimed was set on killing him?

As the days ran on, Brad began to think that the bushwhacking incidents really were figments of the rancher's overheated fancy. There was no reason that he could see for anyone wishing to murder the cattleman, no motive he could hazard at. Of course it was possible that Hank might have fired someone who had harboured a grudge until it festered into a desire to maim or kill. With this angle in mind, Brad began making casual inquiries of the cowhands he happened to be working with at various times.

Old Tom Ward was able to tell him that Allison had chased a man about three years earlier, on account of the way he had ill-treated a horse.

'Clem Duke was the jasper's handle. A bad-tempered bully that everybody was glad to see the end of. But here, son, why the interest in gents that used to work for us?'

Brad had discovered that the old-timer was level-headed and sober. He was a good hand with cattle, and the foreman wasn't troubled much with giving him orders. Brad guessed, too, that Ward could be trusted to keep a confidence.

'I was just wondering, Tom,' he ventured. 'You see, I heard tell that the boss had been shot at a couple of times before I hit these parts. What do you think of it?'

The gnarled oldster gave him a beetle-browed, inquiring stare. 'You're looking for news and gossip, ain't you, boy?'

'I'm kind of curious,' Brad admitted.

'Let it stand at that,' he was advised weightily. 'It's true that Hank was used for target practice a few times. But if you think that some waddy who used to work here is behind it, you're wrong.'

It was Brad's turn to stare 'No fooling? But who would do it, Tom? Who would want Hank out of the way? Why would anybody want him dead?'

'Mr Travis,' the other said dryly, 'did the boss hire you to try and find the answers to them questions?'

'No, he didn't ... I needed a job and he hired me on account of being grateful for saving Glo—Mrs Allison's hide when her team spooked in town.'

'You nearly called her Glory then, fella.'

Heat pulsed into Brad's face and he silently cursed Ward's alertness. The elderly cowhand grinned crookedly.

'It's her name, isn't it?' Brad grunted, trying to retrieve the situation.

'Oh, sure it is, mister, and nobody's saying it ain't. Now listen, you're a likeable young stripling, and maybe I could give you some good advice ...'

'Save it, Tom.'

'Just as you say. You was the one who started throwing the questions. I'm not the rumour-monger of the outfit.'

Brad was obliged to let it go at that. But at least he had been offered some evidence of the bushwhacker being a reality, if it could be called evidence. Only, how to lay hands on the unknown man who wanted Hank Allison out of the way?

Out of the way ...

Brad's mind clung to the words for a while. Supposing Glory was playing fast and loose with someone, and that someone knew he was under suspicion ...

He discarded the notion. Certainly, Clete Baxter was in constant contact with Glory Allison. Clete might hold her hand when the opportunity arose, might call her by name when a slip of the tongue occurred. But the foreman could not be blamed if he came under the spell of the woman. Glory had the power to bring any man she chose to the centre of her web—himself included, he admitted ruefully. Still, it was quite possible that the woman had no real feeling for anyone but her husband. It was plain that she was bored with the general run of things at Bar A. Glory was vivacious, restless; she was of the type that craved the attention of men. But what real harm could ensue from that?

A week after Brad's conversation with Tom Ward, the rustlers struck at Allison's herds yet again, this time at the north-east corner of Bar A range. The rider who brought the news reckoned that another fifty or sixty head had been spirited away, and when Allison led a band of cowhands that included Brad Travis to the scene, they were shocked to find that a cowboy called

Ted Cherry had been shot to death.

Hank Allison was like someone possessed as he bent over the dead herder. He had taken it on himself to post Cherry on his night-hawking mission.

'I had a hunch,' he said hoarsely to the tight-featured Clete Baxter. 'I figured this was a likely place to make a steal, and I was right.'

'You were right,' Baxter agreed coldly. 'But you can see how dead Ted Cherry is, Hank. I thought we had an understanding about posting night-guards. I told you it wouldn't work and just left the men open to attack. We don't have enough hands for that kind of operation.'

'Then I'll hire a bigger crew,' Allison raved. 'And, Clete, who's boss of this outfit anyhow?'

'Does it mean you don't need a ramrod any longer, Boss?'

Allison jumped as if he had been stung at Baxter's emphasis on 'Boss'. He flung his arms out in a furious gesture while his mouth opened and closed like a fish freshly hauled out of water.

'I didn't say that,' he declared finally. 'Anyway, put some of the boys to trying to trail the hellions. Come on and we'll look around for tracks.'

They spent an hour in futile searching, and by the end of that time the rancher had regained control of himself. Baxter waited for a repetition of the order to put some men to hunting the rustlers, but it wasn't forthcoming. Hank Allison had realized the hopelessness of such a task. And these men were cowhands after all, not trackers.

'Pack Ted aboard a horse and we'll take him home,' he directed.

On the way down back through the grasslands he drew close to Brad and spoke in a tone pitched for his ears alone.

'What do you think of it, Travis?'

'Looks like the same pattern, I guess. A small gang. Two, maybe three. No more,

I'm sure. They appear to know where to make a cut.'

'Glad you've noticed,' the other responded with satisfaction. 'Now, you get on with it, mister. At the minute I don't know a damn where I stand, or if folks are with me or against me. You're about the only man I'd trust to stand up for me. It's the reason I hired you, remember.'

'I remember. But it could be a big job, and a long one. And one other thing, Mr Allison ...'

'Yeah?' the rancher urged testily when he paused. 'Don't be afraid to speak your mind.'

'I'm not. You shouldn't get the idea that your men are against you. It isn't true. There's just one or two bad eggs somewhere that'll have to be dug out and smashed.'

'Find them,' was the terse injunction.

Allison rode off to join his foreman and Brad stared moodily at them for a while before addressing the trail ahead of him.

Again he saw Hank Allison in a dark tunnel of his own contrivance, unsure and frightened.

'Who wants to kill him?' he muttered to himself. 'Who's the bushwhacker? Who's behind these steals? Are they the same people?'

On the way back to headquarters he found Clete Baxter watching him covertly, an odd glint in his eye. He would have given a lot to know what the foreman was thinking.

Five

Brad's assignment meant that he was able to get out from under the shadow of Clete Baxter. In many respects he became an independent agent, with the right to come and go as he pleased. Hank Allison made it clear that none of his men was to question where Travis journeyed over the vast tract of rangeland known as Spanish Flat; they were to help the newcomer in any way they could.

At the outset, Clete Baxter objected to the tack adopted by his boss. There was no need for a rider to travel around on his own, in the hope of getting a lead on the rustlers, he said. Clete backed up his argument with the suggestion that the boys would object to what they would undoubtedly interpret as someone being given the licence to spy on them.

'It's what it amounts to, isn't it?' the foreman said to Allison one evening while they were discussing problems in the small office at the rear of the ranch-house. 'You'd better come right out with it if you figure some of our own men are in cahoots with the wideloopers.'

'I didn't say any such thing,' the rancher protested. 'But I happen to know that Travis is a good man at this kind of work. It's the reason I hired him.'

'Oh?' Baxter was taken aback by the admission. 'Your *main* reason for hiring him, eh? You almost sound as if you knew Travis before he hit these parts.'

'Of course I didn't. Don't go jumping to conclusions, mister.'

'I'm just trying to be reasonable, Boss. What makes you think he can succeed where nobody else can? Is there something special about him?'

'Damn it, Clete, quit going on! Do I have to explain every decision I come to, every move I make?'

This was tantamount to showing a red rag to a bull. Baxter scowled for a moment, rubbing the side of his neck. 'If you've got something up your sleeve I need to know about it,' he persisted. 'Or maybe you reckon I'm not doing my job properly?'

Allison kept his temper in check with an effort. 'I'm losing more stock than I can afford to lose, Clete. *I* know it, and *you* know it. It means I'll take whatever steps I think necessary to catch the hellions. And when I do catch them, they'll not take the Oxbow trail: they'll get a short dance at the end of a rope.'

'Don't let Sheriff Adrian hear you talk that way,' Baxter warned through clenched teeth. 'He mightn't like it at all. Anyhow, I can't see this new man doing what a whole outfit can't do. And how can you be sure that Travis himself isn't ...' He let the rest trickle off when a warning glint came into the rancher's eye. 'Well, let it ride,' he finished with a shrug. 'As long as you know what you're doing.'

'I hope I do,' Allison rejoined sourly.

Shortly after the foreman had gone, Glory brought coffee into the office and sat down beside her husband. She draped an arm about his neck.

'Hank, you're taking everything far too seriously. Clete is right, you know. He's a good man, and it has reached the point where he could almost run the outfit on his own.'

'What's that you say?' Allison stared hard at her, something akin to fear on his face. But the shadow vanished quickly when Glory laughed and drew his head against her bosom.

'See! Haven't I told you? You view the worst side of a situation. Kiss me, Hank honey.'

Allison kissed her. He did so without fire, conscious of the absence of that strong feeling that had impelled him to woo and claim this woman in the first place. Sometimes he thought he had made a mistake in marrying someone so much younger than he. Glory was youthful and vivacious; her proper setting would be one of those old southern homes that Allison had left behind at the end of the war, where the nights had rippled with the sound of music and where young men and women danced and flirted while the tinkle of laughter and wine glasses made a mockery of the night hours. But the old south and the old ways were gone forever ...

'I don't know what I would do without you, Glory,' he heard himself sighing. 'You're really all that matters to me in the whole world.'

'Hank, you are so romantic! But so silly as well. And why should you have to do without me? You aren't thinking of going away?'

'Good grief no!' He came back to the moment with a thin chuckle. 'I promised to take you to 'Frisco, honey. And I'll do it, too, by grab! Only, there's so much work to get through.'

'I understand, Hank. I really do understand. And I'm a patient woman, even if I have few other virtues to recommend me.'

'You witch,' he cried, and drew her to him fiercely. A sudden welling of passion flooded into his bloodstream like rich wine and his heart sang with joy and gratitude.

On this starless night Brad found himself too far from ranch headquarters to make it back home before dawn, so he twisted the buckskin through a tangle of scrub and clinging vine to reach a line-house that was located in this lonesome end of Spanish Flat.

Allison had told him to make full use of these outlying camp-sites; they were usually well stocked with canned food: dried apples, peaches and the like. So far, Brad had stayed overnight in three of them.

When the dark hulk of the log building

loomed out of the shadows he dismounted and stripped the horse. He rubbed it down before putting it on a picket-rope close to a spring that was surrounded by a skirting of grass. The interior of this shack followed much the same pattern as the others, and he struck a match and brought a candle from a cupboard. By its light he saw where rats had been busy, gnawing at a flour barrel. They had chewed a chunk out of the strongly-built food cupboard as well, but so far they hadn't managed to break through. That was strange in a way: rats could chew through just about anything.

Soon afterwards he had a fire burning in the old stove and placed a coffee pot on to boil. Then he filled a basin and stripped to scrub himself, finishing off with a shave that left him feeling somewhat refreshed.

So far, he had seen nothing at all of would-be rustlers in spite of a patient and assiduous search in all corners of the Spanish Flat range. At first the routine had irked him, and he had been tempted to ask Allison to let him go back to punching cattle with the rest of the crew. He missed the time-fraying work and the cheerful company, with the occasional game of cards in the evenings. But as the days progressed, he began to savour the opportunity for solitary riding, and he told himself that he was doing a worthwhile job for his boss, and perhaps for the other cowmen in the territory as well.

His main objection to the role he had adopted was the way his fellow punchers had changed subtly in their relations with him. At the outset they had suspected him of being some tough gunslick; they were pretty certain now that he was, in fact, a detective employed by some cattlemen's association, a hardcase, and possibly a killer to boot, who might see a narrow demarcation line between cowhand and rustler—or indeed who might consider the terms synonymous, and who was, therefore someone to shun at all costs.

As he took some jerked beef from his

pack and sawed into a can of tomatoes, he reflected briefly on Clete Baxter's reactions. The foreman resented his presence at the ranch and made no secret of his feelings. Yet Baxter appeared to tolerate the newcomer in some fatalistic fashion, as though he had decided that this new fad of Allison's would soon lose its appeal.

Brad saw little of Glory during these days, and on the single occasion when they met face to face, she had been friendly and cheerful, and that incident in the house when they had been alone together might never have been.

After eating his supper he felt drowsy and smoked by the settling stove until he could no longer sit upright. He went outside to have a look at the buckskin, then spread his blankets on one of the two rude wall bunks, and blew out the candle flame.

The muted sounds of the night beat against his consciousness in pleasant waves: the soft mourning of the wind through the trees and brush surrounding the line-house, the odd stamping of the horse on the green turf, the yap-yapping of a coyote further up in the hills he had spent the day in combing.

The rustle and fall of the ashes in the stove were the last sounds to register before sleep crawled in and claimed his senses.

He came awake with the feeling that something had disturbed him, some noise that was foreign to the natural tenor of things. He spent no time in speculating or waiting, but slid from the bunk and reached out to where he had left his clothing handy. Booted, he lifted his gun gear and buckled the belt around his waist. The shack was windowless, so that there was no way of investigating other than by opening the door. He paused with his hand on the coarse edge of the timber, fondling the cold handle of his Colt, straining to pick up sounds.

The howling of a wolf came in on

a weird and wonderful note, trenchant but full-throated, hinting of hunger and triumphant anticipation. The dim bawling of a cow or calf followed swiftly. The buckskin nickered, stamped a couple of times, and then was still.

Nothing so far to cause alarm, and Brad wondered if the wolf had upset him. But no; his senses were too acute and well-trained to play him false. Some danger lay on the other side of that door. But what shape did it assume?

He let a minute drag by, another. He decided to take the shiftings of the buckskin as his guide. It whickered again, and then he heard the low, crisp popping of a twig or branch being trodden on.

It was time to abandon the waiting game.

He lifted the wooden bolt from its notch and eased the door open carefully, standing now with his revolver in readiness. There was a meagre glow in the sky which he took to be the faint glimmerings of pre-dawn. The breeze was fresh and laden with tree scent and the odours of sage and grass. He could make out the clump of scrub and brush across the way, directly opposite the door of the shack. Nothing moved out there that he could discern.

He took a slow, tentative step into the open, and now the breeze tugged fiercely at his hair and whipped his cheeks. Hank Allison had stopped placing night riders since the death of Ted Cherry, so that if a horseman was abroad it could only be a drifter who had spied the shack, or one of the shadowy creatures who preyed on other men's cattle.

A blur of sound on his right drove Brad into a swinging movement with his six-shooter levelled. He was able to glimpse an elongated shadow a second before something slammed down wickedly on the base of his neck.

His trigger-finger applied pressure instinctively, and he heard the sharp bark of the explosion, but he was sure the bullet spent itself in the earth as he buckled at the knees. He was attempting to lurch groggily upright when another blow took him, coming in from the left, this a hard, booted toe that gouged into his ribs and flung him outwards to the stinking, weed-covered earth. Voices assailed him in a vague snarl of disordered noise, some of the words filtering through to his reeling brain.

'Kill him and be done with it ...'

'No! Not so fast. It might be too dangerous.'

'Blazes, what do you call this caper—child's play?'

'Warn him. That's all. It's what—'

'Shut up.'

The voice gave Brad a clue to where the speaker was standing, and he lunged out at shadowy legs, clutching and wrenching mightily until he was flung back with a hard, contemptuous oath. A boot caught him a sickening blow to the side of the face, and now the world erupted in a Chinese cracker display. Pain lanced and stung, shooting searchingly to every nerve and fibre of his being. The air he managed to drag to his lungs was hot and searing.

He was hauled to his feet, and imagined that his gun was still clutched in his fingers. Dismay swept over him when the truth dawned. Then anger and bitterness swamped him, became a burning hatred directed at his attackers. Retaliation was impossible. Fists rained on his face and neck and chest; they drove him to his knees, when the booted feet took over. He moaned and cursed, frustration bringing harsh sobs from his constricted throat.

A time passed when there was no feeling at all, no awareness of anything. When he opened his eyes at length it was to see streamers of orange and silver and pearl slanting over the east as if someone were busy throwing out ribbons across the sky. Birds cheeped and chorused, and finally he raised his head to look around him.

His tormentors had gone: a long time ago, he was sure. Every nerve in his body screamed its own particular protest when he heaved himself to his knees, and then to his feet. Just standing upright was a victory of sorts. He staggered to the wall of the shack and fell against it, holding on until a spasm of sickness had its way. Later, he made it to the spring and flopped down, letting his head sink into the icy gurglings. All the while he tried to work out who his assailants had been, to understand their reason for riding to the line-house and beating him up.

A snatch of that talk returned in little, tantalising echoes.

'Kill him and be done with it ...'

Then the order to let him live. *'It could be dangerous ...'*

Why could it have been dangerous for anyone but himself? Why had they attacked him if their intention had not been to kill him?

He reckoned there might have been three

of them, but two at least, and no more than three. But who were they? And how had they known he was staying overnight at the line-shack?

The obvious answer to that lay in the probability of them having spent some part of the day or evening watching him and trailing him. It all proved one thing at least: he was a marked man. He was not wanted on this Spanish Flat range. So that he really must pose a danger to someone.

'Maybe they think I know something, that I've found out something that could make things unhealthy for them.'

He considered his reflection in a small section of the water that moved around in a slow, placid circle. It had melted the caked blood on his lips and cheeks, and the cuts were beginning to drip once more. But in spite of the pain that racked his body he believed he had suffered no lasting damage. He felt a sense of achievement that transcended his misery. He must be hurting the rustlers in some way, must be close to discovering their whereabouts or their method of spiriting stolen cattle off the range.

It showed that, if he persisted in his efforts, he could still come up with the answers Hank Allison needed. Of course, if he decided to shrug off that stern warning, the rustlers might finish him off on their next visit.

On his feet once more, Brad realized that the buckskin was missing. He swore long and loudly, not caring much who heard him. Likely the raiders had concluded it would be a fitting gesture to leave him stranded out here, miles from Bar A headquarters.

All in all, the message was blatant enough: he had better clear out of the country while he was able to ride or walk.

After a while he came on his revolver. He checked it for loads before bolstering it. Next, he worked out in a slow, widening circle from the shack, hoping to come on his horse. He soon wearied, and returned to the structure. He got a fire burning in the stove and set a full pot of water on to boil. The sky brightened considerably as he sat on a stool and drank cup after cup of the strong black stuff. He felt much better afterwards and spun up a cigarette, smoking while he squatted in the doorway and tried to decide on his next move.

Without a horse he couldn't get far, and walking back to headquarters was out of the question. There was no other course open to him but to remain at the line-house and hope that sooner or later Hank Allison or some of his crew would investigate this corner of the range.

The prospect was one that had little appeal, but Brad had learnt a long time ago how to make the most of things. Should last night's visitors return, he would see to it that their reception was in tune with their intentions.

He was rolling his second cigarette when

a high-pitched neighing reached his ears. The sound set his heart to thumping rapidly, and he slid his revolver into his hand while he waited. His apprehension turned to relief on spotting his buckskin coming through the brush at a trot, head high and anxious, and burred tail bannering on the morning breeze like a harbinger of hope.

Brad laughed heartily as he called and waved. 'Come on in here, you old reprobate! Say, Buck, you know what I'm going to do to you for skedaddling off like you had one of those burrs *under* your tail—I'm gonna strip the hide off'n you and stake it out on a barn door.'

The horse sidled up to him and went through a little mischievous performance that it might well have been rehearsing out there while he searched for it—butting him with its head and then prancing away and rolling its eyes challengingly.

Brad let it work the whole thing out of its system, and after a while it stood meekly, head dipped, nickering some kind of complaint while he set about collecting his gear. It appeared to understand the trouble he had saddling up and then heaving himself into leather. And when it moved back into the scrub and brush it settled down to a gentlemanly gait, soon being prodded into the general direction of Bar A headquarters.

Six

Brad's arrival at Bar A headquarters around noon caused a stir of excitement. He was spotted by a stable-hand who judged that something was wrong by the way he hung in his saddle with his fingers twined into the reins. A shout brought Hank Allison and his wife from the house, and Glory looked on in horror as Brad was helped to the ground and held upright by Allison and the stable-man.

'What happened?' Glory cried when she had found her tongue. 'Are you hurt, Brad?'

He managed a wry grin. 'Nothing to speak of, ma'am. Darned horse spooked at a rattler and threw me into a pile of rocks.'

But when he and the rancher were alone

in the living-room of the ranch-house after his cuts and bruises had been treated expertly by Glory, he related all that had happened at the line-house. Hank Allison listened with a troubled frown wreathing his forehead. The old anxiety was back in his eyes, and he gave an involuntary shudder.

'Bastards!' he grated. He produced a glass of whisky and stood over the younger man until he had drunk. Next, he lit a cigar and gave it to him. Brad was silent for a few moments while he puffed, enjoying the tobacco even though it stung his lips. Finally, he said: 'What do you make of it, Mr Allison?'

'What do you make of it yourself?' the other countered. 'It could be a move to scare you off this ranch. It could have been some *hombres* wanting to settle an old grudge. Any idea?'

'I'm not sure,' Brad responded truthfully. 'But supposing it was some personal thing connected with me riding for you: who would have it in for me?'

'You had a row with Rusty,' Allison surprised him by saying.

'So you heard about that? But I suppose Clete would have told you. Sure, Rusty and I exchanged a few rough words. But I don't think he'd settle his grudges that way.'

'No, I guess not.' Allison plucked at his lower lip, his brow darkening still further. 'Which points to them being enemies of Bar A. Hell, I wish I could get to the bottom of it ...'

He took a couple of turns up and down the room, evidently trying to find some explanation. Glory rapped on the door and entered. She smiled tentatively at Brad.

'Anything more I can do for you?'

'No, ma'am,' he replied. 'I feel a lot better. I mend pretty fast.'

'All the same, this should be a lesson to you. Don't you know what you ought to do now?'

Hank interrupted her before she could

say any more. He was gaping at his wife with something like disbelief in his eyes. 'What do you mean?' he asked hoarsely.

'I mean that Brad must feel he's had enough of Bar A. I know I'd feel that way if I were in his boots.'

'But I fell off my horse,' Brad protested weakly. 'It could happen to anybody.'

'You might have fallen off your horse later,' she rounded on him, sternness in her tone. 'After the men who beat you up were through with you. Isn't that the truth?'

'Well, I'll be damned!' Allison gulped. He tried to drum up a weak smile. 'I guess there's not much sense in trying to hide things from a woman, Travis.'

'Not when she has two sharp eyes in her head, Hank. You'll have a meal, of course, Brad, before you—leave?'

Brad exchanged glances with Allison. Just then the rancher's brow was thunderous; yet he was reluctant to hurt his wife's feelings.

'I think you're catching the wrong end of the stick, Mrs Allison,' Brad said with a short laugh. 'You seem to think I'm going to pull my freight.'

Her brows arched stiffly for an instant and she cocked her head to one side, much as an impatient adult might regard a slow-witted child. 'You're a fool if you don't,' she said bluntly.

Some compulsion made Allison take her arm and look earnestly into her face. 'Please don't talk that way, honey. Brad's a grown man, if you haven't noticed.'

The mild sarcasm was lost on her. Her eyes locked with Brad's. 'Oh, but I have noticed. What do you think, Mr Travis?'

Brad felt a tide of heat pushing through his cheeks. The very last thing he wanted was to see Allison and his wife at loggerheads, especially over him. The rancher cleared his throat noisily. He splashed a little whisky into a glass, swallowed.

Brad said: 'I need a job, ma'am. I reckon

I'll hang on for a spell.'

'I just hope you won't regret your decision.'

'Brad will eat with us, honey,' Allison said brusquely. 'Is that all right with you?'

'Certainly, Hank. I'll tell Jethro.' She turned and left the room abruptly.

'I've been thinking, Travis,' Allison said when she had gone. 'What would you say the chances are of the rats who beat you up and whoever has been trying to bushwhack me, being out of the same den?'

It was something that Brad was unable to answer. As yet he had no solid evidence of Allison being the object of bushwhack attempts. It could be a story the cowman was putting around to gain his wife's sympathy. But no, that could not be true: there had been evidence from other quarters which added ample weight to the rancher's claims.

Brad studied the stocky man, trying to add things up and arrive at some satisfactory conclusion. It was difficult to know what to think, what to believe. One thing was real enough, however: the beating he had been subjected to at the line-house. Whoever had pulled that trick hadn't done it just for the hell of it.

If only he could hear those voices again, identify his attackers ...

He dined with the rancher and his wife, and during the meal a big effort was made by all three to keep the conversation away from the shadows that were dogging the place. Even so, Brad was relieved when the meal was over and he and Allison were seated on the porch, drinking coffee and smoking fresh cigars.

After a few moments' silence the rancher cleared his throat roughly. 'I've been mulling things over, Travis, and I believe that Glory could be right after all.'

Brad's eyes narrowed. 'Oh?' he murmured. 'You want to fire me?'

'I mean it, mister. You might be better

off if you left this outfit, moved right off the Flat ...'

'If you want to fire me, come right out with it and say so?' Brad told him.

'Hell no!' the other protested. 'I don't want to fire you. As soon as you'd gone I'd be right back where I started. Maybe worse off.'

'I don't see that we've made any progress at all,' Brad argued.

'You can't be sure we haven't,' the older man countered. 'At least the rustlers haven't left their calling card since you came here.'

Brad shrugged and shook his head. 'Doesn't mean a thing.' But then he had to admit that this was not strictly true. 'You figure that my riding around the way I've been doing has kept the wolves from the flock? I'd like to think that it has. So you believe they want rid of me, and that trick was to scare me off?'

'Looks that way. I know I'd be inclined to run if I were in your boots.'

116

'No, you wouldn't, Hank. You know you wouldn't. Anyhow, I'm not pulling out until you tell me to go.'

This appeared to offer Allison enormous gratification. He reached over and patted Brad's knee. 'You're going to stay and help me wipe out that crew?'

Brad's smile was bleak, reflective. 'Mr Allison, sir, the worst thing that bunch could have done was give me a licking. Even if you paid me off right now I'd still hang around until I found them and settled the score.'

'That's just great, boy! But look, what about taking another man along to ride the Flat with you? It's a big slice of country for one rider to cover.'

'No dice,' Brad returned firmly. 'One man can get around quicker than two. One man doesn't need the same cover as two. And you can bet on something else,' he added with a hard chuckle, 'Those sidewinders will never get a second chance to cut me down to size ...'

He took it easy for the rest of the day: he called it licking his sores. Only then did he realize just how lucky he had been. Apart from running the risk of being killed, he could have been permanently maimed. And, as he had told Hank Allison, his attackers would never get the chance to catch him napping again.

He stayed away from the environs of the bunkhouse until it was pretty late. He hoped that news of the incident at the line-house might have been kept from the crew, but those same hopes took a tumble when he finally turned in, needing to sprawl out on his bunk.

A late card game was going on, with four of the crew taking part. Others were darning socks, reading ancient newspapers and mail-order catalogues, or just relaxing with cigarettes or pipes. Brad was conscious of every eye trailing him to his bunk, where he sat down on the edge of the straw tick. The concerted curiosity in their gazes brought a glow of heat to his cheeks.

'Howdy, fellas,' he said. 'How's cattle punching these days?'

'Not as bothersome as fighting off night riders, mister,' Monte Walsh came back with a slow grin. 'Why didn't you send home for help?'

'Wasn't sure if I'd get it,' Brad replied with a cool smile that discomfited Walsh.

Rusty Barnes chipped in. 'Meaning you didn't think we'd take a hand in your grief, Tall Man?'

'I didn't say that.'

'But you meant it,' Barnes accused. He pursed his lips over the pasteboards he was holding, grimaced in disgust, and flung them to the discard. He looked at Brad. 'Maybe you figure us jaspers would rather take a kick at your face?'

'I don't know about that angle, Rusty. I'm just doing a job for Bar A. There's nothing more to it.'

'All right, friend Travis. But if you get into any more trouble than you can handle, do us a favour and shout. If we hear, we'll hustle there fast enough to pick you up out of the mud.'

'That's real handsome of you. I'll remember.'

Brad had thought to turn in so that he might make up for lost sleep and give his body a chance to recover, but the buzz of talk and banter continued, and presently he roused and jammed his hat on, moving to the door again.

'Ain't you staying with us tonight, pard?'

'I'll be back.'

He felt a lot better out under the stars. He was grateful in a way for the blunt but forthright offer of friendship from Rusty Barnes. It showed how a man could make a mistake by jumping to hasty conclusions.

He went as far as the corral again, and the buckskin came to the rails at once, nickering softly. Usually he had a lump of sugar in his pocket, and he fumbled until he came up with a tiny wedge.

'Just a little on account, Buck, old friend.'

He rubbed the horse's nose and patted its neck, then pushed it away to join its fellows. He got a cigarette going and leaned over the top rail, wondering if the aches would ever leave him. He froze when he heard a rustle of movement somewhere across yonder by the corner of the barn. He forced himself to relax. He was on home ground now, safe from attack. It would be one of the boys, probably, storing his gear. Still, when a minute went by with no other movement, he peered through the shadows while a ripple of anxiety coursed along his backbone.

Then a voice came to him, low-pitched and framing some sort of protest. Brad killed his cigarette instantly. That was Glory Allison speaking. She was off there in the darkness, talking with a man: not her husband, Brad felt sure.

All his deep-rooted suspicions regarding the woman came to the fore, together with a keen curiosity regarding the identity of her companion. Why did they have to sneak out here in the shadows to talk? He shrugged, telling himself it was none of his business. But then he remembered that Hank Allison was paying him to keep an eye peeled for anything which didn't fit neatly into the general scheme of things.

The word 'spy' sprang up accusingly, but he thrust the label aside in distaste and turned away, moving stealthily. He made a detour that soon brought him round to the opposite corner of the barn. He peered into the gloom and presently discerned the outlines of the woman and the man. They were so close they might have been a single shape. They were silent now, and no great stretch of imagination was needed to deduce that they were embracing.

Brad buried his teeth in his lower lip and winced from the hurt he stirred to life. He canted his head as the woman spoke.

'Whatever you do, be careful. If he

found out anything he'd kill me. I know he would ...'

The man's reply was muffled, husky. When he tried to bring the woman into his arms once more she backed off, whispering sharply. 'No, don't. I—I must go.'

'It won't be long, Glory. I promise you. And then we'll ...'

The rest was torn away on a hard breeze that whipped along the wall of the barn, rattling a loose shake at the same time. The pair separated, and the woman began walking rapidly in Brad's direction. He swore under his breath, looking wildly about him. He spotted the open doorway of a shed across the way and hurried towards it. He reached the opening and ducked inside just as Glory Allison arrived at the corner of the barn where he had been standing. The woman continued without breaking stride, going on to the back of the ranch-house.

As soon as she was out of sight, Brad returned to the corner of the barn, anxious to discover the identity of her companion. He was disappointed when he found no one there. He felt he really needed to know who had kept that clandestine rendezvous with Glory. He had a strong suspicion, of course, but he wanted to be absolutely sure.

He shifted on round to the front of the barn and halted at the wide entrance where a lantern burned dimly inside.

'Hello there, Travis.'

He swung on his heel, his right hand streaking to the gun at his hip. He forced himself to relax when Clete Baxter brayed a hard laugh.

'Say, you're a jumpy sort of a cuss, aren't you?' Baxter chuckled.

'Sorry, Clete. It's what comes of having a guilty conscience, I guess. Or maybe this whole crazy outfit is getting on my nerves.'

'Yeah, I heard about your trouble at the Brushy Spring line-camp. But I figured you'd be asleep by now. Hank said you'd gone to the bunkhouse to turn in.'

'Lot of noise over there.' Brad endeavoured to sound easy and unconcerned. He could feel the foreman's eyes boring into him. Baxter was wondering where exactly he had been during the past five minutes or so, what he had overseen or overheard. He noticed that the foreman's fingers were splayed above the Colt he wore in a cutaway holster.

'Tell me what happened at the line-camp,' Baxter invited. 'You got a roughing up, I believe?'

'Yeah, I did. But there's not a lot to tell. Didn't the boss give you all the news?'

'Oh, sure he did.' Baxter sounded testy. 'But I've been wondering if you managed to get a good enough look at the coyotes to be able to spot them again.'

'No, I think that's out, Clete. I walked right into a gun barrel that dented my neck. There was no time to see anything but a heap of stars.'

'Quite an experience. And you still don't aim to quit?'

Brad chuckled. 'I know what you're thinking. Staying put makes me out as a prize duffer. But I told the boss I'd give it another whirl.'

'That makes you a nervy critter, Travis. I'll tell you something else,' Baxter went on, a new inflection in his tone, 'I've a strong hunch this kind of hell-raising is nothing new to you. Am I right?'

Brad sensed where the conversation was leading. He decided to cut it short. Clete had apparently satisfied himself that his meeting with Glory Allison remained their secret.

'Time I was turning in, I guess,' he said, not replying directly to the foreman's question. 'Good night, Clete.'

'Wait.'

The sharp-edge tone caused Brad to stare at him. Those splayed fingers hovering above the Colt reminded Brad of an eagle's talons.

'What is it, Clete?'

'You didn't answer me, mister. But I reckon I've got you weighed up, all the same. You're a hardcase, aren't you? Gunslinger, maybe?'

'I don't know what you're talking about,' Brad returned coolly. 'Strikes me this is an outfit of hardcases. What's a gunslinger anyhow?'

Baxter's laugh was intended to be off-putting. 'Look, Travis, you needn't get huffy with me. We've both been around quite a bit. We're gents who know what we want.'

'What do you figure *I* want?' Brad came back swiftly.

'Hell, drop the bluff, Travis. Money's the word, isn't it? Is there anything else in the world. Tell me!' He added on a different note: 'If you can catch Hank's rustlers you'll be doing yourself a really big favour—unless you get yourself killed in the process. Ain't that the truth?'

'And so?' Brad pressed. 'Have you got

some bright ideas about how a drifter might line his pockets quickly?'

Baxter leaned closer and his narrowed eyes appeared to drill clear into Brad's skull. His mouth slanted into a sardonic gash in his shadowed features. 'You catch on fast, Travis, don't you?' he whispered.

'I'm not sure what you're driving at, Clete.'

'It's easy finding out. Come in here a minute.' And when they were in the depths of the big barn, with the lantern throwing a yellow aura about them: 'Would you like to make a lot of money fast?'

Brad's nerves quivered. He had bother keeping the excitement he felt in check. He grinned crookedly. 'Who wouldn't? But you're just fooling me, mister, ain't you?'

'Would five hundred be a help?' Baxter suggested sibilantly.

'You're loco, Clete. How many months do you have to work to earn that?'

'You might be surprised, mister! Now, get back to your bunk, boy. Keep this under your hat and think about it. Think of five hundred all done up in a nice package. Maybe tied up with a ribbon!' He laughed recklessly. 'You could grab that and shake the dust of Spanish Flat out of your pants.'

'I'd be expected to raise dust afterwards?'

'Well, hell, what would you expect?'

'But I kind of like it here on the Flat. I like the tall hills out yonder, and the trees and rivers and criks ...'

'You're the one who's loco, mister. If you hang around here for much longer do you know what's liable to happen to you?'

'Those gents at the line-house ...'

'That's just a start. A sample, maybe. Know something, Travis, those jaspers might take the hide off you next time. Maybe just blow your dumb brains out.'

'Now wait a minute, Clete. I'm not that stupid.'

Baxter punched him playfully in the chest. He raised a hand for silence and listened intently for a moment, then he said: 'We got a deal, pard?'

Brad contrived to look serious and thoughtful. He shook his head slowly.

'What are you trying to say, boy?' Baxter prodded impatiently.

'Wish I could make my mind up, Clete.'

'Damn it, you'd better make it up fast. Don't you want to earn five hundred dollars?'

'You betcha, Clete!'

'Would you kill a man for that kind of money?'

If this shocked Brad he managed to conceal the fact.

'Who?'

'That's enough for now,' Baxter said brusquely. 'One thing at a time. But I'm the one who asks the questions: get it? You think over what I said. Don't wait too long. Then come and tell me what you decide. *Sabe?*'

'I reckon I get your drift.'

'That's just swell.' Baxter was sober

130

now. He eyed the tall man speculatively. 'Watch how you go. I'll see you later.'

He left Brad alone in the barn, but Brad soon shifted outside and returned to the corral. He rolled a cigarette and spent a long time turning things over in his mind.

Seven

Brad slept little that night. While he was reconciled to having to suffer from his cuts and bruises for another few days, a greater irritation plagued him and would not let him sleep. He kept going over his talk with Clete Baxter. There was a cool one and no mistake! Baxter had suggested that Brad Travis might kill a man for the princely sum of five hundred dollars. What sort of creature would make such a proposal? Obviously, the foreman had him branded as a gunslinger, pure and simple: an opportunist who would jump at any chance to line his pockets and further his ends. But what did Baxter have in mind? What mischief was he planning? There seemed no doubt that Clete was scheming something of importance, something terrible.

When sleep finally claimed Brad he dreamed of Baxter and Glory Allison embracing and laughing beside a tree where a man hung by the neck from a rope, and when he went closer to look into the hanged man's face he saw that it was Hank Allison.

On awakening he discovered that the crew had already gone from the bunkhouse. Nobody had bothered to rouse him, and it was hard to say if this neglect sprang from sympathy or just plain indifference. Every muscle in his body protested, but by the time he had pulled on pants and boots and gone out to wash, he felt a good deal easier. His mind buzzed afresh while he soaped and scrubbed, and then scraped stubble from his chin. His first duty was to Hank Allison, and he ought to go to the rancher straightaway and aquaint him of the latest development. By then he had no doubt who the gun victim was supposed to be—Hank Allison himself.

He tried to guess how the rancher would

react to the information. Would Allison face Clete Baxter and demand to know the nature of the trick he was planning, or would he decide to let the foreman carry on with his plot and set a trap for him? Or again, might he not laugh at Brad's story, judging it as a move to discredit the foreman?

Brad pursued this line of thought. He could visualise Hank Allison challenging Baxter, demanding to know if Travis' story were true. He could well imagine the foreman's scornful denial, then his demand that the trouble-maker be chased off the Spanish Flat country forthwith.

Brad was back in the bunkhouse, buckling on his shell-belt, when Clete Baxter stepped in from the early sunlight.

'Morning, Travis,' the foreman greeted stiffly. 'Thought I might find you here. Boss wants you to take a ride with him as soon as you eat breakfast. Got a notion he intends to visit Brushy Spring for himself.'

Baxter appeared cool and businesslike, and Brad could detect none of the excitement he had exhibited last night. It was as if the man he had spoken to in the barn and the man standing in front of him were two different people.

'All right,' he said tonelessly. 'I'll be ready shortly.'

'You didn't find anything over there that might give us a lead on the thieves?' Baxter queried while he eyed him keenly. 'It's what you said anyhow.'

'Not a thing. Can't think why they jumped me, except they intended making a steal thereabouts.'

'It's what the boss figures they might still do. Better watch how you go out there.'

Baxter spun on his heel and started back for the open. Brad spoke after him. 'Clete.'

'Yeah?'

'That thing you were talking about last night ... I've been thinking it over.'

'Oh, that? Just forget it, mister.'

He was gone before Brad could gather his wits, and he wondered just what Baxter was up to. Had he baited some sort of a trap for him last night that he had walked into blindly? Had the foreman been acting under orders from Allison himself, with the purpose of testing the new man for flaws?

Brad shrugged and went on to the mess-hall for breakfast, earning a sullen scowl from the fat chow-wrangler.

'Another couple of minutes and you'd have had to do without breakfast, mister. What do you figure this is—an Elite Hotel?'

'Set it up or keep it,' Brad snapped irascibly. It seemed that nothing on this ranch was what it appeared to be.

His retort drove the cook to silent and hurried activity, as if he realized he had overstepped the mark, and soon a steaming plate of beans, bacon and fried-over spuds was placed on the table in front of him, together with a steaming coffee-pot. The cook lingered in the doorway of his sanctum then, watching him curiously. Brad lifted his head while stuffing his mouth and grinned.

'Barney, your grub gets tastier and tastier. It's a wonder how you do it.'

This was balm enough to eradicate the cook's surliness, and he smiled happily and waddled back to his quarters. Brad ate up and then went out to catch his buckskin. By the time he had saddled and reached the front of the house, a stable-man was holding Allison's horse. The cowman emerged and greeted Brad with unusual cheerfulness.

'How do you feel this morning, Travis?'

'Good as new,' Brad responded with a grin. He affected a grimace and added: 'Well, just about. You mean to go to the line-house where that outfit jumped me?'

'Yes, I'd like to have a look for myself. I spent most of the night thinking about the hellions who did it. I confess I can't figure it at all.'

They set off at a canter, with the new

sun flushing the east with orange and silver that soon brought the colours of the landscape into brilliant life. Hank Allison was a good horseman and kept up the pace tirelessly, so that, by the time they reached the location known as Brushy Springs, both horses were in need of a breather.

'We'll take a look at the shack first,' Allison suggested. 'Just in case some of those rogues have been using it as a hidey-hole.'

He pushed his horse slightly in front of Brad, and the next instant the clamorous rattle of a rifle erupted. The cowman cried out with shock and pain. His horse reared on its hind legs, throwing the rider heavily.

For the space of five seconds Brad's mind was numbed by the suddenness of the attack, and he stared stupidly at the slumped form of his employer on the ground. Awareness asserted itself and he hauled the buckskin around on a tight rein, snapping his revolver to his fingers and earing the hammer back in a single, fluid motion. Next, his angry eyes flashed this way and that, trying to pinpoint the bushwhacker's location.

He fancied he saw movement on a brush-covered ridge and raked the buckskin's flanks wickedly, sending it into a bustling charge that took them across a dried-up creek bed and into a section of thorny scrub. He halted at the bottom of the slope to peer around him, looking for tell-tale signs. As he moved over to investigate a clump of live-oaks the drumming of hoofbeats travelled to him on the hot air, hammering off towards the south.

Brad drove his mount forward, letting it pick its own way across the treacherous terrain. This corner of the range was riddled with pitfalls: gopher holes, rents in the earth that were partly shielded from immediate detection by thick brush, small rocky clefts and crevices that offered challenge and threat to the most sure-footed horse.

Brad swept down a track between two outcroppings of rock that ran on a parallel for a hundred yards before spreading and completely dominating the scene. Here it was necessary to slow and move with the utmost caution. He thought he glimpsed a man bobbing over a hogback ridge and chose a winding goat-path that would give him access to the south side of the hills. But when he hauled in once more on a stretch of rock and sandstone he was met with nothing but the harsh, forbidding landscape baking under the merciless glare of the sun.

Brad swore softly in his teeth, batting the brim of his hat up from his steaming forehead and shielding his eyes with flattened hand to stare this way and that in the hope of spotting the fleeing ambusher. He saw now how Hank Allison was fully justified in his fears. Coupled with this realization came the memory of Clete Baxter's proposition of last night. Had the foreman decided to perform his own murderous chore, or had he hired what he thought might be a more capable gunhand?

He was suddenly anxious about Hank Allison and berated himself for leaving the rancher lying back there. He swung his horse around and went back on his tracks. The possibility of Allison being dead put a tightness into his chest, and he tried to shed the dread that accompanied the stark picture. He had ridden out here alone with the rancher, and that might make subsequent explanation difficult, if not impossible.

The sweat oozed from his pores as he speculated on the probability of this whole thing being part of Clete Baxter's elaborate plot to get rid of his boss and the newcomer at one stroke, and to claim Glory for himself. It was plain now that Baxter had been putting the new man to the test last night, wanting to find out if he was willing to hire out his gun.

'That would really put me on the spot ...'

He pushed his horse recklessly in his haste to get back to the place where his boss had fallen. He heaved a sigh of relief when he spied Allison trying to get to his feet. Hank made it, and managed to stagger a few yards before toppling to the earth again.

'Hold on, Mr Allison. I'll give you a hand ...'

The cry caused the rancher to raise his head. He made another effort to stand, but succeeded only in flopping over on his face. Brad hauled the buckskin to a halt and leaped from his saddle. He had temporarily forgotten his own hurts and bruises, and the movement sent pain flashing along his nerves. Nevertheless, his boss' welfare came first and he went to Hank's horse, thinking he might have a spirit flask in his saddle-bags. He was groping through one of the pouches when a hard clattering of hooves reached him and he spun around, hauling his Colt clear.

Three riders swept up, coming from the general direction of the line-house, cowhands he soon recognized as Rusty Barnes, Jim Perks and Jack Mitchell. They raced to the spot in a wild threshing of hooves and ran sharp eyes over the scene.

Rusty Barnes swore. 'By hell, that's the boss lying there ...'

All three dismounted and approached Hank Allison. Brad had failed to find a whisky flask and now he hurried over to join them. Barnes managed to turn Allison on to his back. He swore again when he saw the blood on the rancher's temple.

'He's been shot! Boss, are you all right?'

'He's dead, Rusty,' Jim Perks proclaimed in a strangled gasp.

'No, he ain't,' Jack Mitchell cut in. 'But he mightn't be far from it.' The cowhand raised his head to put a slit-eyed stare on Brad, and Brad's blood ran cold. 'Better get him home fast as possible,' he said thickly.

'Ahuh! You're sure a nervy polecat, mister, ain't you? Getting the boss out here to—'

'Watch your tongue,' Brad warned him. His jaw dropped when Barnes hauled his six-shooter out and levelled it on him. 'Hey, put that down, damn you, Rusty. You've got it all wrong.'

'Want to bet?' Barnes gritted. 'Get his hogleg, Jack.'

'Nobody gets my gun,' Brad told him. 'If you think I shot the boss you're way off the mark.'

'Get his hogleg,' Barnes repeated. 'If he won't give it up alive, he'll sure as blazes do it when he's dead.'

Brad burned with fury and frustration as Mitchell gingerly relieved him of his six-shooter and pushed it into his own waist-band. Next, Mitchell brought Hank Allison's horse over, and all three of them lifted the cowman and heaved him across his saddle. Allison groaned a couple of times and appeared to be trying to fight his way back to consciousness.

'Take it easy, Boss,' Barnes advised. 'You're in good hands, and we'll soon have you home ... Travis, climb aboard your nag and ride in front of us. We're taking no chances on you getting away. I'd rather see you hung than shot.'

There was little use in arguing. Besides, it would only waste valuable time. His own life depended on getting Hank Allison to headquarters and seeing him regain consciousness so that he might tell the right way of the incident. Jogging out in front of the three punchers on the homeward trail, he reviewed the minutes leading up to the shooting. Allison had wanted to have a look at the line-house first, and had moved away from him. When the shot came, Brad had been behind his boss, so that the rancher might not be able to say with any certainty who had triggered the bullet. Even so, an examination should reveal that Allison had been brought down by a rifle bullet. Or would it? A rifle bullet or revolver bullet could have made the head wound, and it would be hard to prove which weapon was responsible.

The sun was dropping into the west when the ranch buildings came in view. They had halted several times to ease the rancher's position and endeavour to force some water through his lips. Now he hung across his horse like a man already dead. Looking at him, Brad's mouth went tight and dry, and he was tempted to make a break for it. If Clete Baxter had been working to catch him in a trap he had certainly succeeded.

It was Glory who spotted them first as they moved into the front yard. She came down the porch steps and halted, pale-faced and big-eyed, staring first at the cowboys, and then at the form slumped across his mount's saddle.

'Brad, who—who is it?' she wrenched

out when no one offered immediate explanation.

'Your husband, ma'am,' he replied evenly. 'We were riding near the Brushy Spring line-camp when—'

'Save your lies for later,' Rusty Barnes snapped. 'Jack, you get a fresh nag and light out for Oxbow. Find the doc and bring him here fast.'

Glory threw a puzzled look at Brad before rushing to the horse bearing her husband. She uttered a little sob and touched Allison's bare head with her fingertips. 'Oh, Hank ... Why would anyone kill you?'

'He isn't dead,' Brad told her and noted the quick passage of a flickering thought. 'At least, we hope he's not.'

'No thanks to you, Travis,' Barnes snarled. 'Watch your step now and help carry him inside. Will you lead the way, Miz Allison?'

She went up the steps in front of them, trim back bent slightly, passing a hand across her eyes. She directed them into the parlour and indicated a sofa. When they laid Allison down gently he whispered something. His eyelids fluttered open, closed. His face and forehead were stained with blood, most of which had dried. Brad pushed Rusty Barnes aside and kneeled to get a closer look at the wound.

'Please bring hot water and bandages, Mrs Allison,' he said.

'Now, see here, mister ...' Barnes began, only to be cut off by Brad.

'Shut up,' he rapped. 'Please, ma'am, will you hurry?'

'I'll fetch it at once, Brad.'

A tense silence held as they waited for the woman to return. Brad continued to kneel by the sofa while Barnes stood, undecided, at his back, ready to jump at a second's notice.

'He's coming round!' Perks cried suddenly. 'His eyes are opening.'

It was true. Allison's eyelids fluttered

again; then they opened, and he looked glassily into Brad's face. Understanding appeared to hit him and his lips bent in a wry grin.

'It's you, Travis ... You managed to get me home, eh? Do you—still doubt that somebody wants me dead?'

'I reckon not, Boss. But these *hombres* figure I shot you.'

'You! Hell, that's a laugh. Boys, it ... was some damn bushwhacker that we never got a look at.'

'Then Travis is in the clear?'

'You leave Travis alone or I'll have your guts for hoggin strings, boy.'

Glory came in just then with a basin of water, salve, court plaster and bandages. She gave Brad a single probing look before starting in to clean the wound and dress it. Brad felt infinitely weary of a sudden and slipped outside to take a seat on the rocker. He rolled himself a cigarette and smoked it, staring into the gathering shadows.

Eight

Hank Allison had regained consciousness by the time the medico arrived from Oxbow. His examination showed that the rancher had suffered nothing worse than a bad graze, although he had possibly missed death by a fraction of an inch.

'As it is, I think you'll live, Hank. Do you reckon it was some of those cattle thieves that are plaguing these parts?'

'Who else, Doc? But it's not the first time somebody has tried to gun me down. It's got to be quite a habit.'

'But you can't be sure the gunman was really shooting at you,' Clete Baxter interposed. It was sundown, and Baxter had ridden in with some of the other cowhands. He had stood around with Brad and Glory, waiting to hear the doctor's verdict. Several members of the crew were clustered about the front door, likewise anxious to know how serious a wound their boss had sustained. Baxter glanced at Brad as he spoke and Brad wondered at the dark gleam in his eyes.

'Are you hinting that I might have been the target?' Brad asked the ranch ramrod bluntly.

'It's possible, isn't it? You're a stranger that we know little or nothing about. Maybe somebody trailed you here who would rather see you dead than alive.'

A retort sprang to Brad's tongue, but he swallowed it. Unwittingly or not, the foreman had spoken the truth. There was more than one shadow that could be dogging his steps.

'Do you have cause to fear anything like that, Travis?' Baxter nudged.

'It's possible,' Brad admitted, and added: 'But hardly likely.'

'So you can't be sure?' Baxter's mouth warped into a sardonic grin while Doc

Struther ran a shrewd gaze over the newcomer to Allison's ranch.

'Forgive me for sticking my neck out, mister,' Struther said. 'But what Hank has just disclosed is serious. Somebody lying up to kill him? You were riding with Hank when he was shot, I take it?'

Brad nodded. He was conscious of the way Glory was regarding him, and he wished he could read what was in her mind. 'That's right. I was.'

'You're all beating up the wrong track,' Hank Allison observed from the sofa. 'I know I was the target, not Travis.'

'But this strange notion that you have, Hank ...' Glory broke in, causing Brad to glance at her again. 'Where did you ever get the idea that someone wanted to kill you?'

Allison looked as if he was about to explain, but then he changed his mind. It appeared that he had neither the energy nor the inclination to continue the argument.

'You went after the hellion, didn't you,

153

Brad?' he said. 'Do you reckon there was more than one of them?'

'I'm sure there was only one,' Brad responded. 'He's no stranger either, to my way of thinking. He must know every yard of that territory out by the Brushy Springs camp.'

'How come?' Clete Baxter queried. There was a little supercilious smile at his lips just then that sent a wave of anger pulsing through Brad. He wondered what kind of explosion there would be if he told them about the foreman's suggestion that he shoot someone. Everyone would scorn the idea, of course, and Baxter was fully aware of that. He could afford to be cocky or insolent, as the whim took him.

'The gunman knew how to get close enough to the line-shack to take the shot,' he explained. 'He knew he could make a speedy getaway because he's familiar with the country. He managed to out-fox me anyhow.'

Baxter laughed shortly. 'Well, that's hard

to swallow. A gent who has spent weeks scouring every corner of Spanish Flat?'

'What is that supposed to mean, Clete?' Brad asked the foreman.

Baxter laughed again, spreading his hands in mock surprise. 'Heck, you don't have to be so touchy. I don't mean a thing. But the idea that somebody is riding around, trying to gun the boss down, is crazy. Wouldn't you say so?'

Brad met the man's brittle gaze without flinching. He wished he knew the nature of the game he was playing. He had the feeling that he was being manipulated. Did Baxter hope to needle him into speaking of the talk they had had in the barn? Perhaps he did. Then Clete could use it as a knife to twist in the new man. He would pour scorn on the story and put Brad in the role of liar and agitator, so that no one would give credence to anything he might say subsequently.

'I reckon the boss can answer that one

better than I can, Clete,' he answered coolly. 'He's sure his life is in danger, and I'm inclined to believe it's true.'

At this juncture Glory announced that supper would soon be ready for all of them. She asked them to give Hank a chance to rest. 'He has had a bad shock,' she added, leaning over and touching the rancher's forehead with her lips. 'You would agree with me, Doctor?'

'You're right, Mrs Allison,' Struther nodded. 'And speaking of supper, I confess I'm hungry enough to eat a horse, hide and all.'

The remark was intended to lighten the atmosphere, and they all obliged by smiling politely. Brad excused himself and returned to the porch where flies danced and droned in the blade of light that lanced from the window of the parlour. His eyes ran over the white faces of the cowhands who were waiting in the gloom.

'Looks like the boss is going to be fine,

boys. The doc might stay until morning to make sure.'

'Well, that's something,' Rusty Barnes said gustily. 'Travis, have you any idea who the bushwhacker might have been?'

'I wish I had, Rusty.'

'Boss hired you to protect him, didn't he? I hear that's why you're at the ranch.'

Brad answered him with another question. It was something that had bothered him since getting back with Allison. 'How come you fellas were close enough out there to ride in when the boss was hit?'

'What are you driving at?' Jim Perks growled. 'If you're trying to say we had anything to do with it—'

'I'm not,' Brad interrupted. 'But you happened along quick enough to jump at me.'

'Clete put us to scouting that Brushy Springs location for strays, if you want to know,' Rusty Barnes explained. 'Soon as we heard the shot we moved fast to see what was up. Satisfied, Mr Travis?'

157

Brad vouchsafed no answer. He moved past them and edged towards the bunk-house, rolling a quirly as he went. So Clete Baxter had been responsible for the cowhands being in the vicinity of the line-camp. This provided Brad with a piece of the puzzle that might prove helpful. The attempt on Allison's life could have been manoeuvred by the foreman. Baxter had known that Travis and Allison were setting out for the line-camp. He could have given instructions to Barnes and the others with this in mind. It would have been relatively simple then for Clete to station himself close to the line-house and wait for the opportune moment to make his try for Hank. The sound of the shooting would have reached Barnes and his colleagues—as had happened—and brought them on the run, when they would have found Brad Travis standing by their murdered boss.

'A neat set-up,' Brad muttered to himself. Once the finger of suspicion had been pointed at him, the foreman would have accused him of being the killer. Baxter would then have told everyone he had been testing Travis out as a potential gunman, wanting to make sure his suspicions were correct before accusing him. With that kind of evidence, Brad would have been taken to Oxbow and made to stand trial for murder.

But what did Clete hope to gain by killing his boss?

The answer to that wasn't difficult to find: Baxter wanted Glory Allison, and he also wanted control of the Bar A ranch.

Even in the quiet of the bunkhouse, Brad felt a needling of restlessness. He ought to be on the move over that dark range out there, trying to discover who had manhandled him at the line-house, trying to find proof against the man who had bushwhacked Hank Allison.

The cowpunchers drifted in at intervals, and the nightly card games were soon under way. As usual, Brad was asked to join in, and tonight there was more sincerity in the invitation than of late. He refused, stepping out at length and finding his steps bending towards the corral.

He humped his saddle from the barn and brought the buckskin through, saddling and stretching out from the ranch, riding until the night silence enclosed him in an insulating circle, with the lights of the ranch headquarters dim pinpoints in the distance.

He rode in a leisurely manner, almost aimlessly. He savoured the keen touch of the breeze on his cheeks; enjoyed the rhythm of the buckskin's easy swinging motion. It was a rhythm that presently entered his own being, and only then was his mind free and able to function with its old facility.

The moon came up as he rode, unconsciously veering towards the east and north. Tree clumps stood out like menacing wraiths, arms bending towards him. Patches of grass and sage contrived splashes of shadow of a different sort. Curlews slept, and meadowlarks nestled on the earth that retained a generous measure of the day's heat. Everywhere the cattle belonging to Bar A sprawled and dozed, or continued in their dogged grazing. Closer to a stretch of woodland, night-hawks and owls rustled the dark silence with muffled wings.

He was out on the plunging slopes of Spanish Flat when something made him haul hard on the buckskin's reins and sit up, straight and tense, every nerve keyed. He listened, and soon heard the measured plodding of a horse. Then a voice drifted dimly, and behind all that he picked up the protesting lowing of a steer.

The rustlers were abroad again!

Brad realized that he had two choices: he could swing around and head for the ranch as fast as he was able and rouse out the crew, or he could go forward on his own and do what he could to frustrate the outlaws. The first option was the more attractive as well as the most sensible, but by the time he returned with the boys the thieves would have managed to make their cut and be far beyond reach.

His hesitation was momentary. Pinning the point of the disturbance, he back-tracked a little, then entered the trees and made a short swing before venturing into the open once more. Now he was half-way down a grassed slope that dipped to Buzzard Creek. This was where a small herd of steers had bedded, and where the rustlers had decided to make their steal.

Directly in front of him he glimpsed the bobbing rumps of cattle through the moon-silvered shadows. A horse whickered and a shout raced to his ears.

'That's enough, Beck. Get them shifting fast as blazes. Don't let them over the creek ...'

Then there was some sort of commotion and Brad saw a bunch of cattle break away from the main herd and charge in his direction. The buckskin lunged and whinnied. A horseman came dashing along, attempting to stem the runaways. He spotted the stranger and dragged his mount to a skidding halt.

'Look out, boys!'

He sent a shot blasting at Brad, but Brad was on the move by then, trying frantically to evade the storm of heaving hides closing in on him. Another gun banged and the bullet whipped past him; still another weapon opened up, and then he was spurring the buckskin into a driving circle with his own Colt clear of leather and snarling clamorous defiance. He thought the rustlers would make a concerted dash to cut him down, but the leader spun suddenly and pealed a harsh order.

'*Vamoose!* There might be more of them ...'

A shadowy figure drifted between Brad and the moon-bright heavens. A splurge of crimson made a brief blob and the bullet whistled past Brad's face, almost scalding his cheek. He triggered and fancied he saw the outlaw rocking in his saddle. But he managed to pull around and hammer after his comrades.

So far Brad had counted three of them. The leading two scattered on towards Buzzard Creek, splashed through the shallows and bent into the south, shooting behind them as they went. The third man had got himself trapped in the now milling mass of cattle. Brad heard him swearing as he darted this way and that. His horse appeared to stagger and lose its footing, and for the space of a second Brad had him under the muzzle of his gun. But he held his fire and sent the buckskin jumping forward as the rustler lost his seating and fell.

He reached the man while he strove to get to his feet. The cattle opened on either side, blatting and lowing, and Brad left his saddle in a leap, only to tilt into a full-blooded blow from a knuckled fist that rocked him back on his heels.

'Damn you,' the rustler panted. 'Who in hell are you?'

Brad ducked the next wild swing, steadied himself, and delivered a hurtling uppercut that snapped to the angle of the cow-thief's jaw. Down he went in a welter of arms and legs. He tumbled, rolled, corrected his flight, and sprang to his feet. But Brad was in on him before he could gather himself, delivering punch after punch.

The outlaw was strong, wonderfully agile; he was game enough to bear up under the stinging punishment of Brad's lashing fists. But the onslaught soon proved too much and he lost his footing when the strength ran out of his legs. His knees buckled uselessly and he flopped to the earth.

'All—right ...' he hustled. 'Lay off, will you?'

'Get up,' Brad snarled from compressed lips. He was hard put to control an old killer lust. He grabbed the man's revolver and stood above him, legs splayed, his tall, wide-shouldered figure spread against the moonglow like a towering Nemesis.

'What—what do you aim to do with me, mister?' the other choked.

'I've a good mind to kill you. It's no more than you deserve.'

He let the man climb to his feet and told him to mount his horse. The steers had run as far as the bank of the creek, but for some reason they had halted there and were moving around, complaining noisily, sweat rising from their hides in clouds. The sounds of the horses ridden by the rustler's companions had long since faded in the distance. Brad waited until the man was mounted, then stepped aboard his own hull. He had never seen this rangy, blunt-faced character before, but it was possible that Hank Allison or some of his crew would recognize him. In any case, capturing the man was a definite bonus, as he might be coaxed into talking about the rest of the gang.

'What you going to do with me?' he demanded. 'I wasn't doing a damn thing. just riding by when I heard them beeves on the run.'

'Tell that to Hank Allison,' Brad snapped. 'Get moving.'

'Allison?' the outlaw croaked. 'But I thought he was—'

Brad stared at him when he broke off. 'You thought what?' he urged softly. 'That Allison had gone away on a world tour? That he had caught a fever maybe? Or maybe you just figured he was dead? What about that?'

'Hell no! Mister, you sure got a suspicious nature. And you better remember that you ain't got a damn thing on me.'

'We'll see. Move or I'll plant a slug in your lying mouth.'

The outlaw pushed his horse into motion and Brad went after him. Now another idea sprang to his mind and he caught his breath. But he couldn't be sure. He would have to be patient, have to tread carefully. If he was lucky he would soon know whether his hunch was right—when he had a chance to judge Clete Baxter's reactions.

Nine

When he saw the lights of the Bar A buildings the captive rustler panicked. Without warning, he kicked his horse into a hard run, veering away sharply to Brad's left, with the result that Brad was thrown off guard for a fleeting moment. He swore furiously as he swung the buckskin about and sent it galloping after the fugitive, hauling his gun clear as he went.

'Hold on or I'll bore you!'

The outlaw paid no heed. He threw himself low on his horse's neck and urged it forward at breakneck pace, skirting a maze of corrals and speeding on towards a jumble of outbuildings. Someone was watching from the front yard and pealed a yell: 'What's going on?'

Brad squeezed trigger, sending a bullet

dangerously close to the rustler. When another shot followed swiftly, this one even closer, the man evidently had a change of heart about trying to get clear. He dragged on his reins, shouting back at Brad: 'Don't shoot, mister. Don't shoot ...'

'That all depends on you, friend. Now just remember your manners and head back to the yard.'

Brad saw the shadowy figures of cowhands, and querulous calls were flung back and forth. By the time he had herded his captive in at the front of the main building the outlaw was thoroughly deflated.

'Don't let them hang me! Damn it, show a bit of mercy, mister.'

'That depends on your behaviour from now on,' Brad told him. He eyed a cowhand. 'Is that you, Perks?'

'Travis, by hell!' the cowpuncher exclaimed. 'What's the shooting about? Who have you got there?'

'A visitor. See you treat him real nice. And I mean just that.'

Another figure bustled up, and Brad recognized Tom Ward limned in the moonlight. Ward crowed like a triumphant rooster. 'I'll be damned if our pilgrim hasn't raked in the pot ... Who is it, Brad?'

'Bring him over to the house,' was the crisp response.

The racket had roused all the hands from the bunkhouse and captive and captor were soon surrounded by a curious group, everyone talking at once. But when the word 'rustler' leaped into the darkness like a burning brand a hush fell over the yard.

'Is that what this *hombre* is, Travis?'

The question was levelled in a voice as cold as ice. The speaker was Rusty Barnes who stepped forward and clutched at the cattle thief's arm. Without warning, he brought the man to the ground unceremoniously and gave him a hard heave. Brad dismounted and got between them, arms extended.

'Simmer down, boys. Nobody's going to do anything foolish. He's my prisoner, and I'll decide what's to be done with him.'

'Your prisoner!' Barnes echoed scornfully. 'What in hell do you think you are—a sheriff or something suchlike?'

'That's a gent called Pratt,' Monte Walsh enlightened Brad when he had taken a closer look at the outlaw. Pratt's face was a pale blob in the moonlight. His eyes reflected stark terror.

'So you know him, Monte? Name of Pratt? Anything else?'

'Just that he's usually to be found loafing around Oxbow, swilling whisky and keeping to himself.'

'Sib Pratt?' someone else cut in. 'Yeah, I know him. Sheriff Adrian gave him a week in the lock-up one time for busting a bartender that refused him a drink.'

'It's a lie,' Pratt hustled. 'I was just riding around when—'

'That'll do,' Brad growled at him. 'Even

a snake can only wriggle so far, friend.'

A man emerged from the front door of the house and Brad glanced at Clete Baxter. Glory came out behind the foreman and halted on the porch while Baxter thumped down the steps. He demanded to know what the fuss was about.

'I surprised a bunch of wideloopers at Buzzard Creek,' Brad explained curtly. 'The others lit out, but I caught this one. There's a chance they might come back for another try at the herd.'

The news rocked the foreman to a standstill. But his pause was only momentary and he swept the ring of men around the captive aside. Brad watched him, wishing there was more light to read the expression on his face.

'Who is he?' Clete demanded raggedly.

'Don't you recognize him?' Brad drawled.

'Of course I don't.'

'He's a loafer out of town, Clete,' Monte Walsh supplied. 'Sib Pratt.'

'I see ... Look, Monte, you and some

173

of the boys saddle up and go have a look at the creek.'

'Sure thing. What do you aim to do with him, Clete?'

'Lock him up for the night,' Baxter said, eyeing Brad as he spoke. 'I'll take him to the sheriff in the morning.'

'What in blazes for?' Rusty Barnes protested. 'Travis here says he was stealing our cattle. What's the use in catching the rogues if we don't string them up *pronto*?'

This drew a murmur of approval from the others. Brad's hand instinctively went to his hip. Baxter rounded on the crew.

'I'm the ramrod of this outfit,' he grated. 'Anybody who doesn't want to obey my orders can collect his time.' He waited for further protest, and when none was forthcoming he added: 'Saddle horses and head for Buzzard Creek fast as you can. Travis is right when he says they might come back. Good work, Travis,' he went on with a tight grin. 'Better go in and report to the boss. I'll see that this gent is locked up safe.'

Brad nodded without speaking and left them. He took his buckskin to the corral and turned it loose. When he returned to the front of the house the yard was empty. Almost. Glory Allison had appeared again and was framed in the doorway.

'Are you coming in, Brad?'

He mounted the steps reluctantly. Something persisted in nagging at him. He had the feeling that Sib Pratt should not have been left in the care of the foreman. He had noticed Pratt giving Baxter a strange look.

Glory entered the house and he followed her. She chided him gently about walking out on his supper.

'But it seems that you made good use of your time.' She smiled, then became grave. 'Brad, they—they wouldn't dare hang that man?'

'I just hope not. They'd better not touch him. He's of more use alive.'

'Yes, I see what you mean. He might tell us who his friends are. That would be important information right now?'

'It certainly would,' Brad agreed.

He was ushered into the parlour, or sitting-room. It appeared that Hank Allison was expecting him. The cowman looked tired and wan.

'Sit down, Travis. We've got a bird caged, I believe. What happened?'

Brad told him all that had taken place, and at the end of the recital the rancher nodded approval. 'You've justified my faith in you, mister. What did Clete do with Pratt?'

'Said he'd keep him locked up till morning. Aims to take Pratt to the sheriff in Oxbow himself.'

Allison frowned at the news. 'He can take him into town all right, but Pratt's sure as hell going to tell us a few things before he goes.' He glanced at his wife. 'Glory, honey, I'm going to make an effort to get about. I can't just sit around when

176

things are starting to warm up.'

'You'll stay where you are until you're really well,' the woman said firmly. 'Now, Brad, if you please ... I think Hank could use a decent night's sleep after all the excitement.'

'Sure thing, ma'am.' Brad rose, drew on his hat. 'I go along with that. See you in the morning, Mr Allison.'

'Just a minute, Travis. I want you to know that I'm mighty pleased with everything you've done. You'll continue to keep your eyes open?'

There was an inflection in his voice that Brad didn't fail to catch. At the same time he noticed Glory's eyes narrowing a trifle.

'Hank, anybody would think that Brad is the answer to your prayers,' she rebuked gently.

'*Quien sabe*, honey? Maybe he is. Good night, Travis.'

Brad dipped his head to both of them and left the room. He heard the door open and close behind him. He had almost reached the shadowy porch when the woman overtook him in the hallway.

'Brad, you—you're trying to avoid me, aren't you? Why is that?'

The golden hair glistened in the muted light of the hall lamp, and his mind leaped back briefly to that first moment when he had marvelled at the beauty of her hair. Part of her features were in shadow, but the full, soft lips were partly open. Seductive as hell, he thought. His throat had gone tight and dry, and he felt angry with himself.

'I'm kept pretty busy about now, ma'am.'

'I told you to call me Glory when we're together,' she reprimanded in a whisper. 'Have you forgotten so soon?'

'Of course not—Glory.' He grinned woodenly.

She took a step that placed her directly in front of him. The full swell of her bosom was almost touching his chest. Her eyes appeared to haze over a little and his pulse-beat went crazy. He swallowed with an effort.

'Good night, Mrs Allison.'

'Wait!' The order was flat and peremptory. He could feel the warm heat of her breath against his face. The provocative lips were mere inches from his own.

'It's no good,' he heard himself saying huskily. 'Please ...'

'How do you know until you've sampled what's being offered?' she countered, the tip of her tongue showing through her small, white teeth.

The next instant she was clawing at his shoulders with surprising strength and her mouth was questing hungrily for his own.

Brad shuddered at the contact. His blood leaped in fierce response before he gained enough strength of will to thrust the soft body of the temptress away from him. Her eyes oscillated like dancing fireflies.

'Who said you were tough?' she whispered. 'You're not so tough at all. You want me just as much as—'

The hard scrape of boots on the porch steps caused her to break off. Through the doorway Brad spotted the tall, wide-shouldered figure of Clete Baxter. Baxter had entered the hall before he saw Brad and the woman. His face tightened and his eyes darted from one to the other.

'Oh, you're still here, Travis ...'

'Just leaving.'

'Talk to Hank?' His gaze was on Glory as he spoke.

Brad nodded. He eased on past Baxter to the porch. Down in the darkness of the yard, he dragged a long breath to his lungs. His cheeks felt as if they were afire and his blood still raced. He muttered a low curse and tried to pull himself together. He had almost allowed himself to be drawn into the evil web that was being woven around Hank Allison. He was glad Clete had turned up at the right moment.

He found the shed where the prisoner was lodged and discovered Tom Ward prowling around, a rifle cradled in the crook of his left arm. Finding the old-timer here like this was somehow comforting. Ward could be trusted to do the right thing, he was sure.

'Everything all right, pard?' he asked.

'You bet. You done a neat job catching him, Brad. Personally, I'd rather give the critter a hemp necktie than act as his nursemaid.'

'We want him alive, Tom. Remember that. We'll let him stew in his juice, then get him to spill the beans about his pards.'

'That makes sense, I guess,' Ward conceded. 'But I'd be inclined to squeeze the whole damn thing out of him right now.'

Brad was heading on to the bunkhouse when a hammer of hoofbeats cut in towards the front yard. He supposed it was some of the boys returning early from their search at Buzzard Creek, and headed round to hear what had happened. He was in time to see

Clete Baxter emerge from the house with Glory, and he stood back as the first of the cowboys galloped up and dismounted, just out of view, but close enough for him to hear what was being said.

'Well, Jim, you didn't take long to look around,' the foreman greeted the arrival. 'Run across anything interesting?

'Not a thing, Clete. Might be a chance of picking up tracks by daylight, but not in the dark.'

'We'll try again tomorrow.'

The rest of the cowhands streamed in shortly afterwards and clattered to a halt. They waited until Baxter told them he was finished with them, then took their horses round back and off-saddled.

Brad returned to Tom Ward. 'Was thinking over what you said, Tom. I reckon I'll have a pow-wow with this *hombre* right now.'

He was surprised when the old-timer plucked his pipe from his mouth, spat, and shook his head. 'Sorry, Brad. No can do. And don't go blaming me. It was Clete's idea. He said *nobody* was to get near Pratt until he's good and ready to see him himself.'

Brad felt a quick leap of anger. 'But I just want a minute with him. He's *my* prisoner, after all.'

'Prisoner, huh? Know something, boy? The way you say that word makes me think of a lawman. Is that what you figure you are?'

'Tom, you open that blasted door or I'm going to crack you real hard over the noggin,' Brad threatened impatiently.

'Even though I shoot you dead first?' Ward cackled. 'Mr Travis, did anybody ever tell you that your head might be getting too big for your body?'

Brad moved in on him, and when the rifle was brought up on a level with him he batted the barrel down irritably. 'Give me the key. I mean it, you old rooster. Now.'

Ward spat and rubbed the back of his

neck. He started to work the lever of the Winchester, chuckled drily, and placed it against the wall of the shed while he poked for the key.

'One thing before you go in there, boy. He tries to make a run for it and I shoot his fool head off. We got a deal?'

'You've got a deal.'

Brad opened the door and drew his Colt. He took a step into the musty gloom, knowing Sib Pratt must have overheard the exchange. He heard a long, slow intake of breath and glimpsed the shadowy form of the outlaw. He had been squatting on a stump somebody had brought in for a stool, but he stood up quickly and backed off against the wall. A bridle rattled on a peg. A rusted nail gave way and let an ancient Mexican saddle slide to the earthen floor.

'You know who it is, Sib? I'm Travis. You know why I'm here?'

'I ain't talking to anybody,' was the truculent reply.

'You'd better talk to me, you thieving bastard. I saved your neck once, but I mightn't be able to do it a second time.'

'I ain't talking, mister. I ain't done nothing.'

'Don't act stupid, Pratt. I caught you cold. All the jaw-wagging in the world won't get you out of this mess unless you talk to me.'

'So what?' the other snarled in a feeble attempt at bravado.

'So you act smart, lunkhead. Tell me about your pards. How many. Names. Especially the handle of the big fella who tells you to do this and do that. *Sabe?*'

'You're just spitting into the wind, Travis. I ain't no rustler. I ain't got no pards. You can't prove a damn thing against me.'

'Stubborn, ain't he?' Tom Ward had sidled in behind Brad. 'Figured all your cussing might have scared the hell out of him,' he added drily.

185

'Stubborn,' Brad agreed. 'But he's pretty close to the mark, I guess. We take him to town, hand him over to Sheriff Adrian. And you know what, Tom?'

'I know,' Ward said. 'He wins the hand. Takes the pot. Scoots off free as a damn bird. Look ... supposing I took him back there into the brush? I got me a right good skinning knife. That might loosen his tongue a mite.'

'Might be a good idea, Tom.'

Sib Pratt laughed nervously. He cupped his hands to his mouth and yelled shrilly: 'Coupla Injuns are gonna use a knife on me! You hear, you cussed cow-wrastlers?'

Brad threw a bunched fist into his stomach and Pratt doubled, staggered, lost balance, and fell. He lay retching, moaning.

Tom Ward plucked at Brad's sleeve. 'Easy,' he whispered. 'Don't make it wuss than it is. Better simmer down, son.'

He was right, of course. Brad left the shed, locked the door, and handed the key to the old-timer. He patted his shoulder. 'Thanks, Tom.'

'Any time, mister.'

Brad bent his steps towards the bunk-house now and walked in on an argument over proposals about the fate of the prisoner. Rusty Barnes declared that lynching was the only sure cure for cow-thieves. Someone else said a quick shot was the best answer. They kept looking at Brad, trying to drag him into the argument. Then, when he just sat and smoked and looked thoroughly morose, Barnes asked him outright what he would like to do with the man he had captured.

'Turn him over to the law, I guess,' Brad replied quietly. 'Every man is entitled to a fair trial.'

Later, when he lay down to sleep, he kept thinking about Clete Baxter and Glory Allison, wondering how far they would go to get what they wanted. The wry notion came to him that their secret ambitions might prove a revelation to each other as well as to Hank Allison. What guarantee did Clete have that Glory would honour whatever deal they had made, once Hank was out of the way? If she wished, she could tell him 'hard luck' and that he'd better clear off, and there wasn't a single thing that Clete could do about it.

He fell asleep at last, to dream of Glory. He was holding her in his arms, yielding himself to everything the temptress had to offer him. He knew it was all wrong, but he was unable to fight his instincts any longer.

It must have been close to dawn when he came awake with a jerk. He knew there had been an almighty shriek. Then a door banged somewhere. The shriek was repeated, over close to the ranch-house.

Brad swept off his bunk and reached for his pants and boots. He knew in a sudden horrible, revealing flash what had happened. And the blue hell of it was he might have prevented it had he acted differently last night.

Ten

The men were already scrambling into their clothes and Brad met Rusty Barnes' eye.

'What is it, Travis?' the cowhand demanded sleepily. 'Thought I heard shouting.'

'You did. Let's go and see.'

Brad plunged into the grey chill of the morning. A swirling layer of mist cloaked the end of the yard where the mess-hall was located, and he made out the form of the fat cook bending over something lying on the ground. Behind them, the door of the shed where Sib Pratt had been held prisoner, lay open. Brad just glanced at it before stooping to look down the slumped form of old Tom Ward.

'Is he bad hurt, Barney?'

'Reckon not,' the cook responded. He had been offering Ward a drink, and now the old-timer shuddered and twisted violently. He opened his eyes and immediately tried to clamber to his feet. A trickle of blood ran down his forehead. He scrabbled about in a dazed fashion until he found his rifle, then peered into Brad's face.

'Somebody hit me hellish hard, mister. Thought I was a goner ...'

A crowd was gathering, and Brad noticed Clete Baxter coming up behind everybody. Baxter cleared a path to reach Tom Ward. Brad went on to the shed and swore when he looked around.

'What a mess!'

'What's wrong, Travis?'

Clete Baxter thrust in past him, halted abruptly, and took an involuntary step backwards. The rustler Sib Pratt lay in a heap. He had three or four knife wounds in his chest and throat.

'He's been killed,' Rusty Barnes cried in

horror. 'Look at all that blood.'

'Poor devil,' Brad grunted. 'So somebody got to him after all ... Didn't even take the time to make a noose.'

'Whoever it was will answer for it,' Clete Baxter declared vehemently. He stepped gingerly around the body, picked up a bone-handled knife that lay on the dirt floor. He extended it, his features a grey blob in the poor light. 'Who owns it?'

He was met with tight faces and fixed stares. He switched his attention to Brad. 'You ever see this before, Travis?'

'I haven't,' Brad answered coldly. 'And remember, if I'd wanted him dead I'd have killed him before bringing him here. But it happens that I wanted Pratt alive so he could talk.'

Another voice cut in on the garble and they all turned as Hank Allison tramped over out of the mist. Hank still wore a bandage on his head and his progress was somewhat unsteady. Glory trailed behind her husband, protesting at him leaving the house. She wore a robe that clung to her shapely body. She halted a little distance off, looking at Brad.

Brad stepped back to let the rancher into the shed. He watched Allison's features closely, noting how the eyes opened wide, reflecting shock, and then how fear showed, briefly and starkly.

'What rat took the law into his own hands?' Hank demanded in a vibrant shout. 'Speak up, curse you, whoever did it!'

'Take it easy, Boss,' his foreman advised. 'It's what we're trying to find out.'

'Tom ought to know something,' Brad suggested. 'We wanted to keep Pratt alive until he told everything he knew about his friends. But somebody figured that wouldn't be a good thing.'

'What are you driving at, Travis?' Allison queried. 'Spit it out.'

'Whoever used that knife on Pratt had just one thing on his mind—keeping him from squealing on his pards.'

Clete Baxter raised a hand. 'Now, wait

a minute, friend. You're only jumping to conclusions. Anybody could have done it. One of the boys could have done it just as easy as the rustler's pards.'

Brad shook his head. 'I don't think so, Clete. Whoever did the killing knew he was taking a big risk, but he thought it was worth it. He had to knock Ward on the head for a start. You don't do that unless you're playing for pretty high stakes. Wouldn't you say so?'

Baxter had no ready answer. He lifted his shoulders in a shrug and glanced at his employer. Hank Allison looked around in the murk, someone had lit a lantern and brought it in. The rancher handled the shelves fixed to the walls, testing them for some reason which Brad soon understood. There were boxes of nails, staples, odd tools used for woodwork. Everything else in the shed was as it should be, and had not been disturbed. Allison absorbed the scene carefully.

'How do you see it, Hank?' Baxter asked

presently. He sounded anxious, uncertain.

The rancher completed his probing before stepping outside the shed. 'I want everybody over in the bunkhouse,' he announced. 'How are you feeling, Tom?'

'Guess I'm not too bad, Boss.'

Glory had been fussing over the old-timer, and Allison spoke to her. 'Go back to the house before you catch a chill.' And when the woman had gone: 'Can you come to the bunkhouse with us, Tom?'

'Reckon so.'

When they had all gathered inside the building, the rancher faced them grimly. 'It's time we had some kind of showdown here, I guess. You all know the sort of beef-stealing's that's been going on for a long time now. Mine isn't the only outfit to suffer. But each man has a duty to look after his own back yard, and this happens to be mine.' He paused to take a cigar from a vest pocket and strike a match for it. His slow, deliberate gaze ranged over the taut, expectant faces.

'There's something else you all likely know through whisper and talk, and maybe rumour. Somebody is trying hard as blazes to get me out of the way. To kill me. Somebody is bent on ruining my ranch and all that the Spanish Flat country stands for. That dead rustler is an example of the mischief, and the killing just has to be connected with what I've told you. Travis there claims Pratt was murdered to keep his mouth shut. There's no proof either way, of course.'

'I'll say there isn't!' Clete Baxter butted in. 'Boss, are you certain you're not making a mountain out of a molehill?'

'That remains to be seen,' was the dry rejoinder. 'Now, I want to say this to you fellas: if any of you figures the only good rustler is one wearing a rope about his neck or a piece of steel in his throat, and if that same gent went as far as knocking Tom Ward over the head just to slice Pratt up, I want him to speak right now. If he does, I promise that'll be the end of it.'

Baxter started to speak again, but changed his mind. A tense silence came in. Then Baxter could contain himself no longer.

'I still say you're building a hill out of nothing, Hank. We need facts before we can tell exactly what happened.'

'We need facts, sure,' Allison droned. He turned to Tom Ward who was rubbing the side of his neck. 'All right, Tom: let's hear what happened and what you think was going on.'

Oddly enough, the old-timer had little to tell. He had been dozing on a stump at the end of the shed, he said, when he heard a step behind him and tried to bring his rifle to bear.

'Never got a chance to use it, Boss. I seen this dark thing just before I was slugged. I must have passed out right away.'

Hank Allison's lips bent in a grimace. 'You're sure you couldn't recognize this "dark thing", Tom?'

'Wish the hell I could, Boss. Next time I see him I'll be ready for him. You just bet your life!'

Brad spoke out then. 'Did you hear a horse coming in from the range before you were attacked, Tom? If one of Sib Pratt's pards came with a knife honed for Sib, he must have used a horse, don't you think?'

'Damn it, you're right, mister! I mean I would have heard a horse coming in, galloping or walking. I can nearly hear the grass growing.'

'All right, Tom,' Allison grunted. He glanced at Brad, nodding slightly to acknowledge the logic of his reasoning. He addressed the cook now. 'Barney, you were up and about before anybody else. Did you hear anything—horses or men?'

The fat cook shook his head. 'Not a thing, Boss. I was going out for water when I seen Tom lying on the ground.'

Allison heaved a sigh. It was evident that he had garnered all the information he would get. He told Baxter to arrange to have Sib Pratt's body delivered to the law in Oxbow in the morning, with an explanation about what had led up to the killing.

'And, Clete, give Buzzard Creek the once over again by daylight. Don't miss anything.'

'I'll do that.' Baxter averted his eyes from Brad's narrow gaze.

Allison plucked at Brad's sleeve and jerked his head. 'Looks like all your work was for nothing, Travis,' he said when they were alone together. 'Too bad. Look ... when you've eaten breakfast, come over to the house, will you?'

'Whatever you say.'

Clete Baxter waited until the rancher had gone before rapping out orders to the men. He glanced at Brad, his brow darkening. 'You know, Travis, I figure it's funny how you happened to be at Buzzard Creek about the time the wideloopers decided to pay a call.'

'How funny do you figure it is, Clete?'

Baxter shrugged. There was a subtle change in his demeanour now. Brad sensed a strong undercurrent of recklessness that set him wondering.

'Aw, just forget it, Travis. I've no time to jaw with you anyhow.'

He swung away, but was trapped by Brad's fingers digging into his shoulder. Baxter whirled, surprise and anger contorting his features.

'Take your hand off me, damn it.'

'I want to hear how you figure it's funny that I was at the creek when the cowthieves were there,' Brad prodded coolly.

'Five hundred dollars worth, maybe,' Baxter said with sudden, fierce emphasis. 'How about it, Travis?'

Brad hit him. His left fist shot out and struck the foreman just below the left ear. The impact bowled him into a spin that sent him crashing against Rusty Barnes and Jim Perks. Both men caught him and held him, exchanging amused grins. Baxter shook them off angrily.

'That's the worst thing you could have done, Travis,' he grated.

Brad was ready for the countering punch, but in the confined space he had little room to weave out of the way. He took the brunt of Clete's blow on his forearm and then drove in, a lot of his fury finding eager, savage outlet.

For a little while Baxter stood up to him, and they hammered each other energetically, toe to toe. But then the foreman began to weaken. His breath came and went in short, panting gasps. A fast, ripping uppercut from Brad lifted a weal under his left eye; another smashed into his mouth and nose, drawing a stream of blood.

The ring of cowhands watched tensely. A couple of them shouted encouragement to Brad; others called on the foreman to make a better fight of it. They hauled the table out of the way and slid chairs and stools to the bunk section of the building.

Baxter managed to get home with a hefty slam to the pit of Brad's stomach that stopped the tall man, but only for an instant. And when Clete decided to follow up, he tore straight into two vicious hooks that sent him reeling against the wall. He teetered there like a tree struck by lightning, tried to steady himself, failed, and sprawled to the floor.

'Look out, Travis!'

The warning was unnecessary. Brad had already glimpsed the foreman making a desperate grab for the gun at his hip. He moved in and toed Baxter's wrist, eliciting a yell of pain and scattering the revolver from his fingers. Brad drew his own Colt, silencing the noisy spectators. He poked the barrel under the foreman's nose.

'Look at it, Clete,' he hissed. 'This time you can see it, but next time you draw on me you won't see anything but smoke.'

'I'll break you, mister,' Baxter choked. 'I'll ruin your name on this ranch and all through the territory. Just you wait ...'

The impassioned threat sparked a glint in Brad's eye and he poked the gun forward again. 'What are you driving at? Come on and spit it out.'

'Just wait and see.'

Brad left him, backing off to the doorway, then wheeling to pass through. Fury still pounded through his bloodstream like a black poison and he trapped a lungful of air, steeling himself to curb his anger. The day was brightening and ribbons of colour flared along the eastern horizon. He held out for a moment in case the foreman should come after him to renew the fight. But it was Rusty Barnes who followed Brad across the yard. Barnes was chuckling heartily.

'By heck, Travis, you're a packet of dynamite and no mistake. One of these days there's going to be a big bang and this whole outfit is going to be blown to blazes. Clete's fit to be tied about now.'

'He's just a bluffer, and don't you forget it.'

'I know. And it looks like his bluffs going to be called mighty *pronto*. I won't shed tears for him if that happens.'

Brad eyed the cowhand keenly. He sensed subtle undercurrents, and felt sure that Barnes had more under his hat than his red hair.

'I believe you've got something on your mind, Rusty,' he said evenly. 'Like to talk about it?'

The cowhand cocked his head, shrugged, then: 'Heck, I'm no great shucks at gossiping. Let's get some chuck.'

Breakfast was eaten in an uneasy silence. Brad was acutely conscious of the covert looks being slanted at him. Outside once more, he saw Clete Baxter over by the corral. The foreman was talking animatedly with Monte Walsh. Brad went on to the front of the ranch-house, hoping that Allison and his wife had not heard of the fight.

He rapped the door and Hank Allison called to come in. The rancher brought the visitor through to his office and indicated a chair. Brad noticed that he kept patting at his head, where the bullet had grazed him. He was still pale, still worried looking.

'You'd better slow down for a couple of days, Boss,' Brad suggested tentatively. 'That wound could turn out to be worse than you think. I remember one time when—'

'Keep the reminiscences for later, Travis. Glory fusses enough without you starting.' He sat behind his desk and poked two cigars from a box, sliding one in Brad's direction. He stared hard at Brad for a few seconds while his lips formed a question. It remained unspoken, however, and he blurted out instead: 'That Sib Pratt character was cut up by somebody right here at the ranch.'

That rocked Brad, and he was silent for the length of time it took him to find a match and snap it alight with a thumbnail.

He puffed at the cigar, saying through the smoke: 'That's a big mouthful. How can you be sure?'

'You saw the way I had a good look around in the shed, didn't you?'

'Yes, I noticed. I knew what you were looking for. You calculated that if some of Pratt's sidekicks had turned up to use the knife there would have been more signs of a struggle?'

Allison laughed gustily. 'Your lawman's training, eh? Know what I think, Travis?'

Brad nodded, a mirthless smile bending his lips. 'I guess I do. You believe that somebody went to the shed and soft-talked the rustler. Told him, maybe, that he was going to turn him loose. Then, when this somebody was inside with Pratt, he pulled the knife, knowing he daren't use a gun. Pratt put up a struggle, naturally, but the first knife cut did a lot of damage. So all the killer had to do was slash some more. It means that whoever used the knife is a born killer. He enjoyed all that cutting.'

Allison had paled even more. He sank back in his chair and got his own cigar burning. He regarded Brad from narrowed eyes, then spoke slowly, calmly, placing studied weight on each word. 'You share my sentiments precisely. I think you know more than you've told me, Travis. You know something—or believe you know something—that you're afraid to come right out with. But you needn't be afraid to talk. I set you to do a job for me. I'll pay you a fat bonus when all this is cleared up. *But I want the truth, no matter how much it hurts.* Understand what I'm driving at?'

Brad could feel heat thrusting into his cheeks. Under that piercing gaze the heat became a fire. It was as if Allison had been watching when he had taken Glory into his arms and kissed her ...

He rose abruptly. 'I want to quit,' he announced in a low voice. 'Right now.'

He expected any reaction from Allison but a hard bellow of a laugh. It was a scornful laugh, threaded with bitterness.

It lashed Brad Travis like the steel-tipped thong of a bullwhip, and for a moment he quailed like a man whose guilt could no longer be concealed.

'What the hell is so funny?' he barked angrily. 'This place seems to be full of jokers.'

'Funny?' Allison echoed. 'Who said it's funny? It's damned tragic, mister, that's what it is! Tragic and shameful. Isn't that what you'd call it, you low-down bastard?'

'Your—your wife ...'

'Glory,' Allison grated. 'My wife, sure. She got to you as well, didn't she? Don't bother denying it! But you're too much of a moralist to steal another man's woman, even someone as desirable as Glory.'

He was fighting back tears now. He was distraught. He had been putting on a brave front for years, worshipping her while knowing she was no better than a bar-room slut. Trying to convince himself she would change, be loyal to him, devoted to him as a good wife should be to her husband.

Brad had his hand on the door-handle when the rancher snarled at him to wait, to come back and sit down.

'Why talk any more about it?' Brad cried. 'I'm not going to get down on my knees and confess. I'm not going to discuss your wife with you.'

'Who's asking! Look, I hired you. I'm paying you to do my bidding. You'd better see this through, Travis. You think I've been stupid, blind? Well, maybe I was for a while. But I know the score now, better than you do, maybe. I want you to stick to your post, Travis. I've been keeping my ear close to the ground. I've been waiting for you to find out who wants to kill me. I just wanted somebody else *to tell me what I already know!*'

'You know who it is?' Brad demanded incredulously.

'Blazes yes! And so do you, mister. That snake Clete. He wants my damn wife and he wants my damn ranch ...'

Eleven

The next few days were pretty miserable ones for Brad Travis, caught as he was between a desire to see Hank Allison's problem through to the end and his equally strong impulse to take his buckskin across the lush, grassy reaches of Spanish Flat and never look back.

If Allison were man enough to stand on his own feet he would have it out with his wife and his foreman, tell them he knew of the plot they had cooked up, and make them show their hands. A bullet would take care of Clete Baxter, as Hank must surely have concluded during his sojourns in the private hell he had wished on himself. Why, then, did he not finish the foreman off, if not in open fight, then in the sort of sneak rifle ambush the rancher claimed Baxter was trying to set up for him?

Glory was something else altogether. Allison loved his wife in spite of her real and imagined shortcomings, and if Brad guessed aright, Hank would be more than willing to forgive her everything if she would only anchor her affections where they belonged.

'Watch them both,' the cattleman had instructed him. 'Report anything you think might be important.'

Which had brought the retort from Brad that he was no snooper where domestic matters were concerned, and he would not do anything of the sort.

'Then protect me, damn it,' was Allison's harsh rejoinder. 'If you can't do that you'd better collect your time and drift.'

It was all the opportunity that Brad required. At that moment he might have said *'adios'* to the Bar A, and Spanish Flat, with all the related intrigue and skulduggery. But the situation remained a challenge which he was reluctant to turn his back on.

All this passed through his mind as he topped a cluster of small hills on a sunny morning and viewed the Bar A stock that grazed on the rolling leagues of lush grass. On the surface, he was continuing in the role assigned him by the rancher—that of a hunter of raiders and cow-thieves. At the same time he was searching for clues to lend substance to his theory regarding the cold-blooded murder of Sib Pratt.

He had visited the section flanking Buzzard Creek once more as well as the country where the Brushy Springs line-house was located, hoping to come on some helpful tracks; now he was sweeping the northern boundaries of Allison's land, slowly and painstakingly.

The hills gave on to open grassland, and this in turn dwindled off in country that tilted to brush-choked canyons and ragged breaks, the sort of terrain that demanded the utmost bravery and toughness from the hardy breed whose lifelong pursuit was the minding of another man's cattle.

Brad roved the edge of the breaks, nooning at a spot he knew to be called Angel Peak. The place was so named on account of a high, natural carving in the rocks that took the form of the popular conception of an angel. He found a runnel of water where he and the buckskin drank. He turned the horse loose for a spell and ate some of the beef sandwiches which Barney invariably included in his grub pack.

It was a corner of Bar A range that boasted little animal life. So far, he had spotted only an occasional jack-rabbit, the odd lizard and rattlesnake on flat stones, soaking up the heat. Wild roses struggled for existence among the rocks; larkspur and wort flourished, and now and then he caught the mild pungence of loco weed.

His meal finished and washed down with another draught of water, he tightened the buckskin's cinch, replaced the bit, and prepared to mount. His fingers froze over the saddle as someone commanded crisply: 'Don't make a move, fella.'

Brad's first impulse was to duck and swing about with his hand grabbing for his six-shooter, but he resisted the urge. The cool sureness of the voice told him what his fate would be if he failed to comply with the injunction.

'All right, *hombre*, ease back and turn round.'

Brad complied slowly, keeping jerkiness out of his movements, and presently seeing a lanky man in range garb about a dozen feet away. He had placed himself at the corner of a rock bulge, and must have watched Brad arrive and eat his meal. Now another man appeared over on his right, this one short, heavily-built. His meaty jowls were coated with a week's growth of beard. Beady eyes clung to Brad with glittering cunning appraisal.

'He the one you want to see, Beck?' he asked his companion.

'Yep, it's him right enough. Hank Allison's personal private eye. Come on over here, fella, and make sure you keep your wings raised.'

'What's the jig?' Brad wanted to know. 'This is Bar A country, as far as I know, and I'm a Bar A rider.'

'You're pretty quick about making things clear for us, ain't you, mister? Regular honest Johnny. I said to come on over here.'

Caught in a possible cross-fire as he was, Brad could do nothing but obey. The second man moved in quickly behind him and lifted his revolver from its sheath. Brad was turning instinctively when a clenched fist from Beck caught him on the jaw. He reeled and almost fell. A boot-heel was driven against his ribs, throwing him on hands and knees, where he rested, panting painfully.

'You cowardly bastards ...'

This brought a laugh from the one called Beck. His companion made a gesture and told him to take it easy. As far as Brad could see, this was to be a repetition of the night he had been set upon at the Brushy Springs line-camp. They hadn't killed him then, but perhaps this time they would make amends for their neglect. On reflection, he should have gone for his gun at once and taken a fighting chance. But it was too late now for any regrets.

The boot nudged his ribs again, not so hard this time. 'Get to your feet.'

Brad rose unsteadily, grimacing when he filled his lungs with air. The sun dazzled his eyes and he bent to pick up his hat and drag it on.

'Get his horse, Hobie.'

The squat man lumbered to the buckskin. The horse whickered and minced away when he caught the reins.

'Whoa there, you spunky devil. Just like the gent that straddles you, eh? Well, we know how to take the gravy out of critters like you.'

The horse was dragged over, head

ducked, fighting the rasp of the bit. Brad mounted quickly to save the horse hurt.

'Real mannerly now, mister,' he was warned. 'First bad move'll give me the pleasure of shooting the blazes out of you. Hobie, get our own nags.'

The horses had been hidden in a clump of brush and scrub pine, and when the pair were in their saddles Beck pointed along a sun-yellowed escarpment.

'Head down that trail.'

Brad eased the buckskin forward, and the two hardcases rode close behind him. When the land levelled out on a stretch of sand that was studded with mesquite, they switched their trail sharply towards a distant line of timber in the north.

'Where are you taking me?' Brad asked them. 'You'll see soon enough. Keep your yap shut.'

It was an hour before they reached the fringe of trees. Up here the air was cooler and drenched with pine scent. They struck a path that was matted with needles and strewn with cones. It climbed steadily until eventually another, higher bench was reached. Now the bare ribs of the forest floor showed through the brown and green. Great roots threaded the earth like spiny sinews. Birds made shrill protest at the intrusion on their domain and whirred away to the blue-vaulted heavens. A half-hour later the forest closed in again and the aisles became shadowed and musky. Suddenly a hard challenge pealed out of the woods and Beck called an answer.

'It's us, Ken.'

Now a glade opened in front of Brad. A rule shelter constructed of tree branches and covered with canvas formed a store-house or sleeping quarters. Packs and gear lay here and there. Ken turned out to be a rangy, pock-faced man, and at sight of Brad he raised the rifle he held a trifle higher while his narrow, grey eyes snapped and blinked.

'Is this the stranger?' he demanded, the tone of his voice marking him as the leader of the outfit. When Beck replied with a confident nod he snapped: 'Get down.'

Beck and Hobie dismounted at once, then clawed Brad from his horse with the ferocity of a couple of Apache bucks. Ken snarled at them to go easy.

'He's only one man, ain't he?'

'A hell of a big one, Ken, and he's caused us plenty of bother as it is, what with breaking up that fandango at Buzzard Creek and—'

'Shut up,' Ken told him. He strode over and halted short inches from the set-featured captive. 'You're the gent that trapped Sib Pratt and took him to Allison's ranch, ain't you?'

Brad made no answer, and a bony hand flashed out and cracked against his cheek.

'Talk, you damn whelp.'

'I disturbed a bunch of rustlers,' Brad said coldly. 'It's what I'm paid to do. I caught one of them and brought him back to the ranch.'

'And then murdered him,' Ken thundered. He struck Brad again, almost scattering his senses. Brad was lunging at his tormentor when a revolver muzzle bored against his ribs.

'Go on, mister, and see where it gets you.'

Brad snatched a gulp of air to his lungs. His face ached, and he was sure that a couple of teeth were loose.

'I didn't murder your pard ...'

'Who did then? News got to Oxbow that a widelooper was brought to Allison's headquarters alive, and that somebody knifed him during the night.'

'That's what happened all right. But you're stupid if you think I did it. If I'd wanted your man dead I could have killed him before I took him to Bar A. I wanted him to talk, then brought to town and given a fair trial.'

'He's bluffing, Ken,' the one called Hobie broke in hoarsely. 'Don't let him fool you.'

'I'm not easy fooled,' Ken snapped back. 'But the idea was to bring him here so he could sing. Well, he's sung, even if it ain't a good tune.'

'He's bluffing,' Hobie insisted. 'He just changed his mind about handing Sib over to the law and stuck a knife in him.'

Brad remained silent under the concerted stares of the three. His life hung by a thread, and the first sign of weakness would have, them pumping slugs into him.

'How about it, big fella?' The eyelids were jumping and blinking.

'I'm telling you the truth.'

'Who killed Sib then if you didn't? You must know that much at least.'

'Whoever killed him didn't want him to tell Allison what he knew,' Brad replied in a low, gusty voice. 'We think it was somebody who works at the ranch. A renegade who was in cahoots with the rustlers. The killer got scared and decided to close Pratt's mouth for keeps.'

'Baxter!'

The name leaped out of Beck before he could help himself, and suddenly an icy tension pervaded the very air. Ken's muddied gaze swivelled to the speaker. The eyelids steadied, then came down like hoods.

'You've got one hell of a big mouth, Beck.'

'Sorry, Ken. But what does it matter? We've got this gent here and he can't tell anybody. I was for killing him that night at the old shack. You should have let me. Do it now and be done with him.'

'I ride along with that,' Hobie declared, nodding heavily. 'Let's do it right now.'

'Wait, you lunkheads,' Ken grated. 'You're ready to jump without seeing where you're jumping. Get some rope out and tie him. We'll keep him right here for the time being. We might need an ace up our sleeves when it comes to dealing with that Allison *hombre*. Anyway, I want to think it over for a while.'

It was evident that Beck and Hobie were

against the idea, but just as apparent that Ken was not to be argued with. 'All right,' Hobie said. 'You stay here with Travis and leave Baxter to us. We'll get in touch with Clete. We won't say anything until we get him here, then brace him about Sib.'

Ken shook his head. 'Forget it. Simmer down a while and let me think. Trouble with you gents is you ain't got enough brains to hold your hats on. Stir that fire and make coffee. Fix Mr Travis up first with a rope. Strikes me like he could be as slippery as an eel.'

They were anything but gentle with the manila ropes they used. They secured Brad's ankles and arms, then an end of rope was passed around the bole of a tree.

'Set there and take it easy.'

Beck stripped his buckskin and put it out on a picket rope at the far side of the clearing. A handful of hay was pulled from a sack and tossed to the beast. Brad's gear was stacked with another saddle beside the canvas-covered shelter.

When the coffee was ready, Ken brought a cup over to Brad, giving him enough rope to bring his bound wrists up so that he could use his hands. The outlaw grinned sardonically.

'Sorry we ain't treating you exactly like an honoured guest, Mr Travis. But you're welcome all the same, 'specially for bringing us that piece of news. You ain't lying about Sib?'

'Why should I lie?'

The day dragged slowly. Brad's limbs soon became cramped and stiff. He asked for a smoke, and Beck lit a cheroot and poked it between his lips.

'You can see how we're nice friendly folks, fella. Wouldn't hurt a fly. Haw, haw!'

'Quit your damn play-acting,' Ken snapped at him.

Some time towards evening the three held a whispered conference, and shortly afterwards Ken and Beck saddled horses and rode off through the trees. Ken's parting words were directed at Hobie.

'Watch him well. I want him the way he is for a while. *Sabe?*'

'Sure thing, pard.'

Hobie took his rifle to a spot across the glade, where he was directly opposite Brad bunched under the tree. He fished out a pipe, loaded it with tobacco, and was soon puffing grey streams into the air.

'Ever smoke a pipe, friend Travis?'

'Makes me sick.'

'Yeah? Well, you make me plenty sick. If I'd my way I'd bore you and have done with you. Maybe you're just trying to put Clete in bad.'

'How long has he been working with you fellas?'

Hobie stalked over and drew the flat of his hand across his face. 'Don't get smart with me, punk. What do you figure you are? Now just set there and count your lucky stars.'

The evening advanced, and with the

encroachment of the deeper shadows, Brad began to work furtively at the bonds that held him. Hobie kept the fire burning, but just fed enough wood to maintain a glow. He was probably fearful of attracting a wandering lawman or traveller.

At full dark the rustler, who had plainly been getting more restless with each hour that passed, began to stride back and forth across the clearing. He talked to himself occasionally, and now and then he would stand in front of Brad while a queer light glittered in his eyes.

Brad got the feeling that Ken and Beck were long overdue, and that the outlaw was getting apprehensive. Hobie disappeared into the woods for a while, and when he returned he squatted a little way back from the fire where he would not throw a shadow. Next, he tucked his rifle under his arm and began scouting the clearing, occasionally stopping in front of Brad and staring down at him. He passed no remark and Brad remained silent.

It was plain that Hobie's nervousness was getting close to danger point, and he might be tempted to clear off on his own, making sure to kill his prisoner first.

The moon was lifting over the spreading arms of the trees when Brad succeeded in slackening one of the knots loose on his wrists. His success caused his heart to pound with excitement, so much so that he was certain the outlaw must hear the wild hammering and be warned.

Twelve

After another hour Hobie's anxiety was really getting the upper hand. The more nervous the outlaw became the more Brad feared for his safety. He could tell by the way Hobie kept looking at him that he was contemplating shooting his prisoner and clearing off.

By this time Brad had succeeded in working both hands free, and he was resting his muscles before starting on the knots that secured his ankles. His wrists were chafed raw and his fingers ached under a dull numbess.

Finally the rustler swept across to him, a blocky, threatening shadow against the surrounding gloom. The barrel of his rifle glinted in the dim light cast by the fire.

'I'm getting out of here,' he said thinly.

'Something must have happened to Beck and Ken.'

'Go right ahead, Hobie,' Brad urged, endeavouring to keep his voice cool and steady. 'If they come back I'll tell them you're off in the woods somewhere.'

Hobie stooped over him and showed his teeth in a scornful grin. 'You figure you're a funny man, don't you, mister?'

His legs were close enough for Brad to reach out and grab, only the risk would be too great. Better to try and humour him for a little while longer.

'It's all the same to me, friend. Me, I'm a dead duck, no matter how you look at it. You hold all the top cards.'

'You never said a truer thing, mister. I'm gonna blast you right now. Ain't a damn thing else for it.'

'You're sure a scared critter, Hobie, ain't you? Say, I believe that's sweat on your brow. It is, by heck! You're afraid of me, even though I'm lying here hog-tied.'

Hobie struck him with the back of his

left hand. Then he jerked the rifle up. 'If you're a praying man, you better get started.'

'Listen,' Brad whispered suddenly. He watched the way Hobie gave a wild jerk. The man's nerves were frayed to pieces.

'What did you hear?' he croaked.

'A horse. Don't you hear it? Coming up through the trees.'

'Hell, might be some of your pards from the ranch,' the rustler yelped. 'But they ain't gonna get you alive.'

'Why don't you simmer down, Hobie? Use your brains for a change. It just has to be Beck and Ken. The Bar A boys would never dream of coming into the timber. They've no errand here. Anyhow, I don't show up at headquarters for days at a time, so they wouldn't be looking for me.'

He could almost read the thoughts passing through the outlaw's mind, the frenzy of indecision that raked him.

He turned away from Brad and crossed the clearing once more, disappearing into the trees. Brad began working feverishly at the ropes holding his ankles. The buckskin nickered, sending alarm streaking along his nerves. Now one foot was free, but already Hobie was slouching out of the dark tree boles again.

'You didn't hear a damn thing,' he growled. 'Something has happened.'

'Where did they head to?'

'To see if—' The outlaw broke with a snarl of impatience. He cut over to his own horse and lifted his saddle and gear. It seemed as though he had reached the end of his tether. He would wait no longer for Beck and Ken to turn up.

Brad managed to tug the last strand from about his feet, and it seemed as if Hobie had chosen that very second to whirl on him, poking the rifle forward threateningly.

'You're planning something, damn you,' he cried. 'Ain't you?'

'That's a joke,' Brad retorted scornfully.

'I'm lying here like a turkey trussed up for the pot.'

'No fooling? Let me take a look at that rope ...'

Brad tensed, praying that his cramped arms and legs would not prove utterly useless when he made his move. Hobie was stooping over him when a horse whinnied away down in the woods. The sound caused the rustler to jerk upright. He laughed hysterically.

'Here they come! Damn me, they made it after all.'

His back was to Brad at that moment and Brad heaved himself erect and sprang forward at the bulky shadow. Hobie choked in alarm and tried to bring his rifle to bear. But by then Brad's right fist was crashing down on the side of his neck. Hobie groaned, swore, staggered. He retained his grip on the rifle. The sound of the approaching horses was getting louder by the moment. Brad's legs were almost nerveless. He teetered sideways when Hobie rammed his elbow into his stomach. Then his hands were clawing for the rustler's waist and his fingers encountered the bone haft of a knife.

He snatched it free of its sheath as the stocky man drove a vicious blow at his chest, knocking the breath out of him. The rifle was swinging up once more when Brad sprang with the ferocity of a cougar. The rifle roared and the bullet raged past Brad's cheek. He plunged the knife into Hobie's shoulder, drawing an agonised scream of rage. He freed the blade and struck again, this time for the neck. Another scream erupted that soon dwindled into a strangled coughing and gurgling. The full weight of Hobie's body sagged against Brad, so that he was obliged to move aside and let it fall to the earth.

A cry lanced out of the wooded aisles; it was accompanied by the drumming of hooves on the soft turf.

'Hobie, what's wrong? What's going on?'

Brad stooped and relieved the dead rustler of his six-shooter. He jammed it into his own holster. His limbs felt heavy as lead now that the pins and needles had stopped jabbing him. He lumbered over to fetch his saddle and gear, and moved to the buckskin. Hooves threshed in the undergrowth. A horse whistled, and a man swore. There were two men there at least, and they just had to be Beck and Ken.

The yell again. 'Hobie ... you all right?'

Brad's fumbling fingers had finished tightening the cinch, and he was trying to find the stirrup iron with his toes when the first man entered the clearing.

'Hold on there!'

Brad paid no heed. He spurred his horse and it leaped forward, appearing to sense the great need for immediate and speedy action. A revolver roared and a bullet snarled off through the timber. Another weapon chipped in and the night shadows were shredded by the sharp lancings of angry flame.

Brad made no attempt to return the fire. His energy and concentration were required for his escape bid. He flung himself low over the buckskin's neck and sent it racing into the trees. They soon struck a wide aisle where Brad pushed the game mount to even greater endeavour. In short minutes he heard the clamorous din of pursuit, the harsh yells and curses of the two outlaws. The roar of their guns smote his ears like thunder-claps. Sweat oozed to his forehead and coursed down the planes of his face. The tree scent was heavy, cloying; it appeared to press in on his lungs, stifle his breathing. The forest thickened, and soon the tall tree boles represented hostile bars, impeding him, intent on imprisoning him.

For half an hour he probed deeper into the timber, not too sure of direction, but always bearing towards dark rock shelving that kept tilting to what he hoped would prove to be open country. For a long time he heard the crashing of the rustlers' horses in his rear, but finally, when he hauled up on a ridge that was open to the star-dusted sky, he realized that they had either lost his trail or given up the chase.

At length he emerged on a sloping outcrop of rock and was able to see dark, brush-covered benches dropping below him. He came on a stream and made another halt to drink and water his horse. Afterwards, he eased his pace to favour the buckskin which had served him so well, and presently he entered a shallow ravine which, in turn, gave outlet on to the grass country.

In spite of everything he had been through, Brad felt he had accomplished quite a lot today. He knew now beyond any shadow of doubt that Clete Baxter was in collusion with the raiders of Spanish Flat. The foreman's greed had been instrumental in causing him to play both ends against the middle, a game that was, to say the least, a risky one at the best of times. He was aiming to do away with Hank Allison so that he could win Allison's wife and the rich package that would go with the woman. But Baxter had not really analysed Glory's motives, nor had he looked to what a future might hold where outlaws and killers could force his hand if they so decided, threatening to reveal him to the law in his true colours unless he continued to play the cards they dealt. No matter how he chose to look at it, Brad had to brand the foreman a rank fool.

Brad knew that the rustler gang had been composed of four members—not including Clete, whose job it would be to help with the planning of their forays. Two of the outfit were dead, and if the men called Beck and Ken had any sense, they would read the sign and make tracks out of the country.

The next step, as Brad saw it, was to confront the foreman with the evidence he had garnered and take him to Sheriff

Adrian in Oxbow or call him out and shoot him.

He found another canyon, secluded, and with a spring bubbling out of a cluster of moss-covered rocks. Here he halted, deciding to pass the night at the location. And when dawn broke, he was already in his saddle and striking on out of the hills.

He discarded his original intention of heading for Allison's ranch and showing himself immediately. He closed in on the environs of the ranch layout right enough, but scouted around until he saw the crew set out for the day's work. It was a blustery morning, with a nip in the air, and when the sun pushed above the eastern horizon it had an orange aura, as if presaging a storm.

Brad was puzzled and a little disappointed when he noted that Clete Baxter did not ride out with the men. He settled down in a clump of cottonwoods and smoked, letting an hour go by before cutting in towards the ranch buildings from the rear.

He encountered no one on the way, and took his buckskin to the barn where he gave it a thorough rubbing down, watered it, and left it with a feed of grain. He soused himself under the pump at the drinking trough and dried as best he could on his bandana. Next, he angled on over to the mess-hall and poked his head around the doorway. The cook's heavy brows arched at sight of him.

'There you are now! So you didn't clear out after all ...'

'Clear out?' Brad echoed. 'Somebody been telling tall tales about me, Barney?'

'Looks that way, mister. But here you are, large as life.'

Brad frowned as he straddled a chair and the cook hustled to his kitchen to fetch him some breakfast. Barney elucidated when he returned.

'Story goes that you got tired of the way

things were panning out here and pulled your freight.'

'Well, that's a lie for a start.'

'Glad to hear it. You can bet Hank'll be pleased to see you ... Them eggs might be a trifle overdone, Travis.'

'They're fine. I—' Brad broke off, raising his head to see Barney staring at his hands and wrists. 'Just a couple of scratches I picked up. Tell me, pard, who put the yarn about that I'd pulled stakes?'

The cook fingered his left ear. One of his golden rules was never to repeat gossip because it usually turned out to be ninety per cent plain rumour. He sighed and shrugged expressively. 'I heard Rusty ask Clete about you, and Clete allowed you'd be half way out of the territory by then.'

'Clete, eh? One of these days Clete's crystal ball's going to get him into a heap of trouble. He around, Barney?'

'Haven't seen hide nor hair or him since yesterday.'

Brad was silent until he had finished

eating. Then he plundered a tobacco sack from his shirt pocket and rolled a cigarette. Barney, the barrier down on his natural taciturnity, was all for plying him with questions. Brad evaded direct answers without being too abrupt, but he was soon driven outside again, and he headed for the main building.

As he crossed the yard a voice called from the direction of the corral, and he turned to see Glory. She was dressed in riding skirt and jacket, with a flat-crowned hat clamped firmly on to her golden hair. She had been about to open the gate to bring a horse through, but she hesitated, then took a few steps towards him. Brad closed the intervening space, cold-eyed and stern-featured.

'Morning, Mrs Allison. Getting set for a ride?'

She looked surprised to see him, he thought, and he wondered if she might be disappointed as well.

'I—I was told you had left us, Brad.

Hank has done nothing but rant and rave since the news reached him.'

'Gossip,' Brad amended curtly. In different circumstances this woman could have twisted him around any finger she chose. 'I suppose Clete started it?'

'Well ... yes, I think he did. But you—you look as if something has happened to you? Did you run into trouble?'

'Plenty. But that can keep. Do you know where I can find Clete?'

A slow flush lifted into her cheeks. Still, she was well practiced in handling awkward situations, and she endeavoured to meet his fiery gaze without flinching.

'I believe he went to town yesterday on some errand,' she replied. 'Hank's been thinking about hiring more riders, and he sent Clete to put the news around. But Brad,' she added with a change of tone, 'why are you looking at me like that?'

He glanced around him before answering. The yard appeared empty of life. A few chickens crowed round back somewhere; a dog barked. 'You were going for a ride just now,' he said coolly. 'Mind if I come along?'

A frown clouded her brow, but was soon gone. 'But shouldn't you see Hank first of all, tell him that you're back. Shall I go and tell him?'

'Never mind,' he told her. 'We won't be going very far.'

'Brad, you look as if you're carrying the whole world around on your shoulders.'

'No more than half of it.'

Her saddle was draped on the top post of the corral, and he brought out the horse she wanted. He went back to the barn for his own gear and cut out a roan for himself. The woman was silent as they left the cluster of buildings and galloped over the flats. Two miles took them beyond a long ridge where the ranch headquarters were hidden from view. Glory jerked when Brad, who was riding behind her, spoke her name.

'Yes?' She turned in her saddle and he could see that shadow back again. Consternation had put a tautness at the corners of her mouth. She forced a shaky laugh.

'You don't call this a ride, Brad. Come on and I'll give your roan a real race ...'

'Wait a minute,' he said. 'You've given me a big enough race as it is, Glory. Reckon it's time you were easing up so I can catch my breath. Might be a good idea if you did the same.'

Slow anger replaced her worry, and the regard she put on him became a challenging glare. 'I don't have to remind you that you're acting very strangely, Mr Travis. Would it be too much if I asked you to explain what this mysterious trip is all about?'

'It's about you, ma'am,' Brad replied thinly. 'About you and Hank. And maybe about Clete Baxter as well.'

Her eyes flashed daggers at him. 'Clete doesn't mean a thing to me,' she flared.

'Is that what's troubling you?'

'Does Hank mean much to you?' he countered.

She pushed her horse closer and he thought she might lash out at him. 'It's none of your business. Is that what you came out here to discuss? If it is, I'll thank you to mind your affairs and leave me to look after mine.'

She swung her horse around suddenly, applying the quirt she carried on her wrist. Brad thrust the roan forward and managed to grab her reins, close to the bit. She screamed furiously and tried to strike him across the face. He trapped the hand and twisted until tears came to her eyes. He caught the quirt, released it, and flung it from him.

'You're nothing but a brute,' she accused. 'I've done my best to be nice to you. I thought you were a gentleman underneath all that—'

'It takes a lady to bring out the best in a gentleman,' he informed her evenly. 'And that, Glory, is something you can never hope to be.'

She exploded violently then, trying to get at him with her clenched fists. They wrestled while the horses reared and plunged, grappled with each other, lost balance at the same time, and toppled to the earth in a heap. Brad found himself on top of the woman and held her for a moment while she writhed and trembled beneath him. Fear had taken over, and she raised a pale, wide-eyed face to him.

'Brad, please ...'

He released her and rose to his feet, not bothering to lend her a hand. The horses had quietened and stood a little distance off.

'I want to say something to you, ma'am, and I want you to pay real close heed. If you hanker for Clete Baxter, then hit the trail for Oxbow and clear out of the country with him. He's all yours, except he tries to push his luck any further. I know that you and Clete have planned to do away with Hank, that you want the Bar A and everything that goes with it. Well, ma'am, you just can't have all that. You can't have Hank's life for a start, because I'm here to protect him. And in case you don't know, your precious Clete has been working with a bunch of rustlers all along, stealing Bar A stock as well as anybody else's they can get their hands on. Did you know about that?' he added with grim satisfaction when he saw how her face blanched.

'Oh, you're a liar, Brad Travis, a dirty liar! And you've got it all wrong anyhow. I don't want to kill Hank. I don't want Clete ... Please, Brad, how can you be so cruel to me?' Tears streamed down her cheeks. She attempted to clutch his arms, but he pushed her off. His features were stone-hard, without sympathy or mercy.

'Sorry, Glory, but if there's one thing I can't stand it's a two-timer. They're nothing but rank poison for everybody else.'

He left her and swung aboard the roan horse, and when he rode away her cries were ringing in his ears, only now she was cursing him.

Thirteen

Hank Allison was out and about, a fresh bandage on his forehead, when Brad took the roan horse on to the tamped earth of the front yard. It was evident the rancher had heard that the new man had been back earlier. Surprise and relief flooded his face as he waited for Brad to dismount.

'Say, where have you been, Travis?'

'Where?' A wry grin touched Brad's lips. He saw how he was being subjected to close, uncertain examination. Allison asked him to show his hands and wrists, remarking that Barney, the cook, had noticed how he looked as if he had been having a row with barbed wire.

Allison whistled softly then. 'Cruel bastards! Tell me about it.'

'You got a drink inside, Boss? I had

breakfast right enough, but my innards crave something to settle them.'

'Come to my office. Hey, you Zeke ... take care of this nag, will you?'

A roustabout came to take the roan away and Brad followed Allison over the porch and into the cool, shadowy hallway. Brad paused there for a moment, searching the country rolling away from the front of the layout. The clatter of hoofbeats round back touched his ears. Someone was galloping off. Allison stepped outside to have a look, but was unable to spot the departing rider.

'Who's that?' he queried hoarsely.

'Set up the whisky.' Brad told him. 'And take a solid jolt yourself.'

On reaching the cowman's office Brad dropped on to a chair and waited for the drink. He made no comment when a cigar was pressed on him as well. He tossed off the spirit and struck a match for the cigar. Hank stood over him, and Brad nodded to the chair behind the big desk.

'Might be better if you take this sitting down,' he said. 'I guess it's going to hurt you more than it hurt me.'

The cattleman sat down obediently, spreading gnarled hands before him. His face was pale under the white track of bandage, the cheeks were oddly gaunt and haggard.

'All right, Travis, spit it out. I know you've got something on your mind. Otherwise you wouldn't have swallowed that whisky like it was the last drink on earth. You've something solid to report at last?'

'I reckon.' Brad puffed at the cigar. He could hear the drumming hoofbeats of the rider who was heading away from the ranch. He pushed the regret he felt aside; he had supped his fill of that medicine, and each dose made him a little weaker in ways, but stronger in others.

'Did you see who left just now?' Allison asked in a taut whisper.

'Don't need to look.'

251

'It was Glory, wasn't it?'

'I reckon.'

The rancher's shoulders slumped. One of the big hands clenched until the veins stood out like bunched cords. He fisted the desk-top repeatedly until the wood vibrated.

'Easy, Boss. That won't do any good.'

'What—what happened?'

'I ran into rustlers,' Brad explained slowly. 'There were three of them. With Sib Pratt they made a gang of four. About the size we figured. The contact man brought the total to five.'

Brad paused and heard the hard gush of air from Hank Allison's lungs. This was probably the worst moment in his life. He was being told something he had suspected—for a long time, likely. But he had wanted somebody to say it for him, to put it into words he could not ignore. He raised pain-clouded eyes to the younger man opposite him.

'Tell me his name.'

'I don't have to. You know who it is. But you kept turning your back on the truth. You can only do that for a little while, Hank, then—'

'The name, damn it, Travis!'

'Clete Baxter.'

'Damn him! *Damn him!*'

Allison heaved himself out of his chair. He strode up and down, clenching and unclenching his fists. Brad continued talking.

'You know I never cottoned to the job of spying,' he said. 'Not the kind of spying you expected me to do. I know you got the notion that your wife wasn't playing a square game. You believed she might be in love with Baxter, that they might be planning something behind your back. But you could have spared yourself a good deal of the grief if you'd faced up to the facts at the beginning.'

'What in hell do you mean, boy?'

'You thought Glory might be in love with Clete. But that was wrong for a start.

253

I happen to know that Glory's the kind of woman who'll never really fall in love with anybody. She'll flirt here and there, and how can you blame her? Life at this place was pure misery for the woman. You were blind if you didn't see it. A liar if you say it wasn't so. If you'd wanted to keep her, you should have taken her away for a while, to California maybe. Maybe back east to some of the big cities, Chicago, New York. You should have shown her a good time, and she might have settled down afterwards to being a cowman's wife.'

Brad stopped speaking. Allison looked out through the window of the office. He was likely seeking for things he would never find now. His eyes were empty, haunted. His voice was hoarse, hollow: the voice of the defeated.

'She always talked about seeing 'Frisco ... I kept putting it off. There was always too much to do, and I never really trusted Clete to look after my interests when I wasn't around. I've been a fool, mister, the worst kind of fool. But wait! Clete ... Has she gone off him?'

'I can't answer that.'

'How do you know he was working with the rustlers? How do you know it was Clete who tried to bushwhack me?'

'You said so yourself, remember?'

'I want to hear what you've found out. Tell me.'

Brad related his capture by the cattle-thieves and the journey to the hideout in the woods. He explained how he had discovered that Clete Baxter was the raiders' contact man at the Bar A.

'They know Clete murdered Sib Pratt to keep him quiet. I was pretty sure of that at the time, but now I know for a certainty.'

'And you had to kill another one of them to get away?'

'It was him or me. They would never have let me go alive. And you can be sure they'll hound Clete to even the score for Pratt. Clete overstepped himself there, I reckon. It's a queer old world, Boss, isn't it?' he added with a wry smile.

'Why did Glory leave? I—I should have gone after her ...'

'If you'd wanted to, you'd have lit out at once. You hired me to do a chore, so I did it. When I get going I don't do things by halves. I braced your wife about Baxter. I told her if she wanted him she'd better make tracks fast, and that both of them had better leave the country.'

'You'd no right to do that, Travis. You gave Clete and that—that damn woman a clear run for it? Baxter's my meat, mister: so is Glory. She's still my wife, and by heaven I'll show her she can't get away with this. I'll kill that bastard Clete, and I'll kill her as well ...'

The last was screamed at Brad, and Allison tried to brush past him to get outside. Brad restrained him, and they wrestled back and forth. At length the rancher weakened, and Brad pushed him down on to his chair where he sat, panting and blowing, face red as fire, eyes staring wildly.

'I'll kill them both,' he bleated. 'No matter where they go. No matter what they try to—'

'Happens you mightn't have to look too far,' Brad broke in, trying to mollify him. 'I've weighed up a couple of things. As I told you, Glory doesn't love Baxter or anybody else. If she did love anybody it was you, at the beginning. Just now she's thinking of her own skin. And you can bet that Clete's first care is for himself as well. When Glory finds him in Oxbow she's bound to throw everything I told her about him helping the wideloopers right back in his face. If she does that, Baxter will do one of two things.'

'What?' Allison demanded. His voice was scarcely recognisable now. Murderous hatred swirled in him like a black tide, drowning logic and reason.

'He'll either hit the trail out of the country at once, and alone, no matter what else you imagine,' Brad explained. 'Or he'll come back here and try to brazen things out. Oh, yes, he's capable of doing that! He still sees me as an outsider, a stranger meddling in things I don't know much about. You might as well know that he took me for a gunman, Hank, somebody who'll hire my gun to the highest bidder. What would you say if I told you he hinted he'd pay me five hundred dollars to kill someone?'

'Me?' the cowman choked.

'Maybe. Most likely. But he decided to leave that angle for the time being. But he'd still jump at the chance to rub my nose in the dirt. So you see, he might be tempted to try and mend his fences. He'd like to have Glory, and he'd like to be sitting right there in your chair.'

'He's a worse bastard than I figured he was. But—but what about Glory?'

'She's a woman, Boss, no matter what else she might be. The way I see it, she'll come to her senses, and maybe head back here too. She might get down on her knees and beg you to forgive her. I don't know. But she's too weak to do much on her own. She likes to have somebody around she can turn to and lean on when she's scared.'

'You've got this all sized up, mister.'

'You paid me to use my brain as well as my brawn, Hank.'

Brad helped himself from Allison's bottle and waited for a nod to fill up the rancher's glass. But when Hank got the drink he didn't want it. He lay back in his chair, his eyes darting restlessly over the ceiling. He was drawing pictures there, trying to assimilate all that Brad had found out and what he surmised.

Brad wiped a layer of sweat from his brow. He had almost convinced himself with his story. Of course Clete Baxter wouldn't have the guts to come back and face the music. When he realized that he was caught out in the open and branded a friend of cow-thieves, he would pull his freight in no uncertain manner. And the woman would probably go along with him, in spite of any revulsion or contempt she might harbour for the renegade. What else could she do?

Brad didn't really care what either of them did. If the pair cleared off at once it would be the best solution, as far as Hank Allison was concerned. Hank didn't need a man like Clete around, nor did he need a woman like Glory. Both were poison of the most deadly variety. Even without Glory's presence at the ranch, Clete Baxter would still have stolen Bar A cattle. He might have gone on for years lining his pockets and playing his secret role of renegade. He had likely been doing so since the very beginning.

As for Glory, if she hadn't decided to cheat with the foreman, she would have cheated with some other cowhand drawing Hank's pay. At heart, she was a trollop, with a trollop's avidity for money and all the luxuries she believed money could buy.

If she was deserving of sympathy, it was not in Brad's heart to offer it.

Hank Allison would suffer for a while; he would pine for a while. But he would learn to live with his pain, and after a while it would stop plaguing him.

'I wonder if you're really right, Travis,' Allison got out at last. He had regained some semblance of self-control and reached for the drink which had been poured. 'Supposing they did get the nerve to come back, the pair of them ...'

'What you'd do then has to be your own decision, Boss. But the best course is to sit tight until the mud clears from the pond.'

Allison took a stiff drink, wiped his mouth. His eyes were moody. 'I can tell you one thing for sure, mister: if Clete comes back, I'll have it out with him. I'll bring him out to the yard there and give him a chance to go for his gun.'

'Don't forget that he might kill you.' Brad was fast becoming tired of the whole business, tired of having the cowman cry on his shoulder. Why couldn't he work things out for himself? He wasn't stupid. And how could he even consider the notion that Clete and the trollop would dare show their faces again?

'He can try, Travis, but by hell I'll get him before he downs me.'

Brad managed to get away from the office finally. Clear of the house, he brought a cool draught of air to his lungs. He was tempted to saddle up again and hit the Oxbow trail, hoping to find Clete Baxter still in town. He would call the foreman out and put a couple of .45 slugs into his head. That way, Hank Allison could walk straight once more, even if he might never forgive Travis for doing that part of the dirty work.

Brad resisted the temptation. There were times when it was best to let the dust settle on the trail. Then, when it cleared, it was easier to look around and make a sensible assessment.

By morning the dust should surely have settled, even in Oxbow. But if the problem of Baxter and Glory still remained, there would be nothing else for it but to meet the challenge head on and try to purge the air with gunsmoke.

Fourteen

Dusk fell and the crew drifted in from the range in twos and threes. Brad suspected there would be plenty of rumours flying around the supper table when the cook's tongue got going. Barney was right at the hub of things and knew—or guessed —pretty much everything that went on at the Bar A headquarters.

Brad headed for the mess-hall when he knew the meal would be well under way, but he still walked into a battery of questions. Had he run across any more rustlers? Was it the cattle-raiders who had given him a hard time? Had he managed to get to grips with them? The most important question was kept to the last. Where were Clete Baxter and Glory? Because it seemed that both of them had disappeared.

It was left to Rusty Barnes to put a direct query to Brad. 'Is it true that Clete and Hank's woman have run off together?'

'Put a sock in it, Rusty. That kind of talk won't do any good.'

'But is it true, pard?' the cowboy persisted.

'Say, if you're so dad-blamed curious, why don't you go and ask the boss himself?'

After eating, he returned to his earlier vigil at a spot away from the main building where he could remain unnoticed, but where he was still able to watch the Oxbow trail in case Hank Allison took it into his head to set out for town after all. It was full dark when the rancher emerged from the house and moved across to him.

'Hope you're comfortable there, Travis,' he observed drily. He sounded as though he had managed to pull himself together. 'No sign of them getting back?' he added on a lower note.

'Still plenty of time, Boss. Give them a bit more rope.'

'Do you really think she'll come back here?'

'I reckon,' Brad lied. 'I'll eat my hat if she doesn't.' He rolled a cigarette and struck a match for it. Allison left him and slouched over the yard to the bunkhouse. He was there for some time, and when he appeared again Brad had changed his position so that the rancher could not readily spot him.

He was able, nevertheless, to see Hank mount the porch and sit down on the bench along by the window. Once, Jethro, the house cook and handyman, came out with a tray on which were a bottle and glasses. A shaft of light glinted on the bottle as Allison poured. Then the rancher cupped his hands about his mouth.

'All right, Travis, quit playing possum and come and have a drink. You could do with one, I guess.'

Brad crossed over and joined him,

grinning sheepishly. 'You're a cute old fox, Boss.'

'Once upon a time, Travis, I was sensible then, too. But not any more. Getting old, I suppose.'

They sipped their drinks for a while in silence, and presently Allison cleared his throat roughly.

'Whatever happens, mister, I want to thank you for your help. Take this and put it in your pocket.'

Brad squinted at the envelope being forced on him. He made no move to accept it. 'What's that?'

'Call it a small token of my gratitude. Go on, take it and don't look at me that way. You've earned it. Likely you figure I'm big enough and ornery enough to take care of my own chores. Well, right now I am, mister, and I'm saying you can take your nag and light out any time you please.'

It was a tempting proposal without doubt, but Brad shook his head. 'I'm in no hurry. Unless you're telling me to go?'

'I'm telling you nothing. But you've done your job, and I'm satisfied.'

'Happens I'm not,' Brad rejoined tersely.

It looked as if this might provoke a retort from the rancher. His lips framed a question, but he chewed it back. He said instead: 'I suppose the boys are talking over there?'

'Cowpokes like to chat. What about it?'

'They might have more to talk about soon,' was the weighty response.

'Can I ask you just what you mean, Hank?'

Allison laughed. He poured another drink for himself and poised the neck of the bottle over Brad's glass. Brad shook his head. He sat smoking until the older man decided it was getting chilly and he'd go inside.

'You don't have to hang about,' he told Brad. 'I don't intend doing anything rash.'

'Glad to hear that, Boss.'

'Know something, mister? I like it better when you call me Hank.'

Brad grinned and took the hand that came out of the gloom. 'Don't worry too much, Hank. Your wife will come home.'

'You figure?' the cowman said wearily. He stood there, a broad, blocky shadow, a tangle of greying hair lying across his forehead. It seemed that a shiver ran through him. 'Glory might come back here, Travis. But she won't be my wife. And she sure as hell won't be coming home. This is no longer home to her.'

Brad let it ride. He took a turn about the front yard, the back yard. His hearing was tuned to catch any sound coming from the town trail. None came. He wondered what he was waiting for, what he would really like to happen. Glory to return to Hank? He didn't know; he wasn't sure. All he knew was what he would be inclined to do himself if he were in Allison's boots ...

He went to the barn and brought out his blanket roll, then found a sheltered spot at the end of the main building. He sat down and draped a blanket about his shoulders. He heard a rumble of thunder in the distance. A shaft of distant lightning forked the sky out westerly. He never remembered the moment when he dozed off.

He awoke with the dawn dew on his face; it coated his blanket in a grey dusting of moisture. Strands of gossamer linked him to the wall he leaned against. He stirred and brought a basin of water to the bench, where he soaped, washed and shaved. He used the rough towel he carried to dry himself. A breeze funnelled along by the corral, whipped around the barn, and played coldly on his skin. He dressed quickly and went round to Barney, helped himself from the coffee-pot that must never have cooled since the day it had been bought. None of the crew had put in an appearance yet, and he handed the cook a piece of advice.

'I know you're not a gossip, Barney. Most cow-camp grub-wrastlers would talk the wooden leg off a fella. But you must have dropped a word here and there that got the boys wondering what the hell was going on. Get my point, Barney?'

'I hear you well enough.' Barney kept on rolling out his breakfast dough. He had no intention of admitting to spreading rumours.

He fed Brad at length, and then Brad cut across to the house, where he was admitted by Jethro who, in turn, brought him along to Hank Allison. The rancher looked slightly puffy around the eyes this morning, but there was a bright, determined glint in the eyes themselves. Allison was buckling a heavy gun-belt around his waist.

'Mind saddling a horse for me, Travis?'

'Course not, Might as well saddle a couple when I'm about it.'

'Just as you please.'

They rode away from the ranch buildings while the crew was still at breakfast and forked out for the trail leading to Oxbow. Glancing at his boss, Brad got the impression that he had somehow gained in height. He sat, straight-backed and upright in his saddle, eyes frostily fixed on the road winding out before them.

The heat of the new day was beating down on them by the time they reached the outskirts of the cowtown and sent their horses chopping through the baked dust of the main street.

They were on a level with Sheriff Ben Adrian's office when the lawman stepped out of the doorway and called to Allison.

'Hank, hold on a minute.'

The rancher halted reluctantly, impatience working through his face.

'I'm in a hurry, Ben. What is it?'

'You tell me, Hank. What in blazes is going on out at your place? There was another rustling scare?'

'Some,' Allison conceded meagrely. 'How

did you get the news?'

Adrian looked for the double edge, but when he was satisfied that the query was guileless he answered: 'Saw Clete Baxter in town yesterday morning. Clete said he was looking for new men. Mrs Allison arrived later, and—'

'Know where she is, Ben?'

Adrian had been studying the cowman closely, detecting the pressures that were building in him, working to the surface. He slanted a sharp glance at Brad Travis, but Brad averted his gaze.'

'Know where Glory is, Ben?' Allison asked again.

'Yes, as a matter of fact I do, Hank. Least I think I do. She booked in at the hotel. But ...'

The rest fell on empty air. The rancher had already pushed his horse into motion, and Brad Travis was hurrying along at his side.

'Now wait a minute,' Brad was saying anxiously. 'You can't just—'

'The hell I can't, boy. Who says I can't? Go get a drink, or a mug of coffee at the cafe.'

'I'm damn well staying with you,' Brad grated. 'I've got your money in my pocket and I'm going to see this through.'

'Please yourself. Come along if you want to.'

They racked their horses at the hotel rail and the rancher clumped on into the lobby. He stirred the clerk from some book work and demanded to know which room Mrs Allison was in.

'She's in number six, Mr Allison sir, but she told me not to let anybody disturb her. She said—'

'Save it, son.'

He was already on his way to the stairs, and when they reached the upper hall he turned to Brad, a strange, impish smile making his face almost boyish.

'I can handle this fine, Travis.'

'If you don't pull any tricks,' Brad qualified grimly.

Brad stood aside while the cattleman approached the door numbered six and rapped sharply. There was a long wait before the door opened and Allison jammed a boot into the narrow gap. He spoke softly for a moment and then was admitted. Brad stepped back against the rail of the stairway, releasing a hard breath and mopping his brow. He searched for the remnants of his cigarette makings.

Five minutes dragged by, ten. Brad was beginning to think that everything was panning out fine in there, so that there was no reason why he should not retreat to the lobby. Then a woman screamed. It was the most awesome sound he had ever heard, and his blood ran cold.

He was lunging at the door when a gun banged, then again. A wail of despair ran through the building as the door flew open under his boot.

The scene brought a ragged curse to his lips. Glory Allison lay across a bed, face twisted horribly, eyes staring fixedly. The haft of a knife protruded from her breast. On the floor, her husband emitted a low, tortured groan, shuddered violently, and was still. Hank had been shot through the head. The smoking revolver was still clutched in his coiled fingers.

Brad looked closely at both of them for a minute, then backed into the hall. He felt a hard knot of sickness in the pit of his stomach. Room doors had been flung open, and he found himself looking into a half-dozen frightened faces.

'There's a mess in there,' he choked. 'Don't go in.'

Down in the lobby, he was making for the street doorway when Ben Adrian showed. 'What's the matter? I heard shooting ...'

'Looks like Hank stabbed his wife and then shot himself.'

'Hell's bells!'

Brad went on along the street, his thoughts in hectic confusion. If only he had known what would happen. He thumped an awning post with his fist, venting his frustration. But how could he have known? How can you ever tell what's going on in another man's mind?

He was suddenly conscious of someone approaching the hotel at a fast walk, spurs jangling dully, little spurts of dust coming from his boots. He also noticed two men on horseback across the road who looked vaguely familiar. The man on foot rocked to a halt when he recognized Brad. His facial muscles writhed with surprise and fear.

'Hell, it's you!'

As Baxter screamed that, he was going for his revolver. At the same time one of the men on horseback called: 'What about us, Clete?'

Both of them had guns drawn, and both began blasting at Baxter while Brad whipped his own Colt clear. Finished with the Bar A foreman, the men on horseback brought their weapons swivelling to Travis who, by then, was triggering calmly and deliberately, with no prancing horse beneath him to spoil his aim. His first bullet took the rustler called Ken in the chest, and Ken's mount reared and threw him into the road. Brad ducked behind a stout wooden column as the one called Beck fired frantically. Then Beck brought his horse sweeping into a tight circle, intent on making a run for it. Men and women darted out of his path like frightened quail. Brad sank to one knee, took careful aim, and squeezed trigger once more.

The raider screamed and rose high in his stirrups. His horse reared and plunged, flinging the man out in a flying tangle of arms and legs. Beck was dead before his body settled in the dust.

Finished, Brad told himself bleakly as he came out from behind the column. He stood, looking down at the bodies of the dead rustlers for a long time, puzzling the onlookers by shaking his head slowly from side to side. Then he bent his steps towards Carmody's saloon, telling someone that Ben Adrian might find him there.

Adrian had better make his move pretty *pronto*, however. A drink and a short rest, and Brad Travis would be leaving this Spanish Flat country behind him for ever.

Other DALES Western Titles In Large Print

ELLIOT CONWAY
The Dude

JOHN KILGORE
Man From Cherokee Strip

J. T. EDSON
Buffalo Are Coming

ELLIOT LONG
Savage Land

HAL MORGAN
The Ghost Of Windy Ridge

NELSON NYE
Saddle Bow Slim

Other DALES Western Titles In Large Print

BILL WADE
Dead Come Sundown

JIM CLEVELAND
Colt Thunder

AMES KING
Death Rides The Thunderhead

NELSON NYE
The Marshal Of Pioche

RAY HOGAN
Gun Trap At Arabella

BEN BRIDGES
Mexico Breakout

This Large Print Book for the Partially sighted, who cannot read normal print, is published under the auspices of

THE ULVERSCROFT FOUNDATION